TOCABAGA 4

THE TALOS WARRIORS

THOMAS H. WARD

TOCABAGA 4:

The Talos Warriors

THE TOCABAGA CHRONICLES

by

THOMAS H. WARD

ISBN-13: 978-0692221891

ISBN-10: 0692221891

Transcendent Publishing
www.transcendentpublishing.com

JUNE 18, 2025

It is the year 2025 and major improvements in warfare have been developed over the years. During the Afghanistan War the military starting using drones to spy and kill targets from 10,000 feet in the air. If a drone can be produced to kill the enemy then it is possible to make a walking robot, or so called android. The idea of an android started with Greek mythology when the king of all gods Zeus, ordered a giant man be made of bronze.

A giant bronze android named "TALOS" was made by a god named Hephaestus following the orders of Zeus. In Greek legend Hephaestus was the son of Zeus and Hera the queen of all gods. Hephaestus was the smiting god and blacksmith for all the gods. He made all the incredible weapons used by the gods such as, the winged helmet and sandals used by Hermes, Achilles armor, and Eros' bow and arrows, to name a few of the more famous items. One could say that Hephaestus was the father of robots.

According to Greek mythology TALOS protected a woman named Europa in Crete from pirates and invaders. Europa was a Phoenician woman of extreme beauty and Zeus was in love with her. TALOS would circle the island of Crete three times a day and throw large boulders at ships that approached the island thereby keeping any invaders at bay.

Secretly the Federal government working with the NSA (National Security Agency) has developed a new and even more dangerous combat weapon. Now there is an Army of Droids called RCCDs' operated like drones by a controller or droid master sitting in a room far away from the dangers of battle field. In fact they are walking robots that have no brain, no sense of right and wrong, only that of its master controlling this monster.

Rumor is these RCCD (Remote Controlled Combat Droids) machines can see in all directions in daylight or darkness using radar and thermal imaging. These android soldiers along with flying drones could be a formidable force even for the Army Rangers. They are big standing 8 feet tall at about 1000 pounds. They can carry all most any type of weapon. They do not need to eat or sleep. They are dangerous, very dangerous and offer only death to those who oppose them as they have no heart.

We call these androids "THE HEPHAESTUS ARMY" or "BOTs" for short. We know some day they will come for us. We are getting ready for the battle.

I am Director of Security for Tocabaga Island. I live here along with 556 other Patriots, we are fighting to keep our freedom, keep our homes, and keep our families safe from the evil forces gone wild. Tocabaga is a sanctuary or safe haven, if you believe in the Constitution, the Bill of Rights, and are of good moral character you are welcome here. I do not reveal the full names of the people living here in case the Feds happen to come upon these chronicles. Read my story and tell others what has happened here. Pass it on; it may save your life.

We are waiting for you to contact us by email to find out where Tocabaga is located. Sending us an email is your first step to Freedom. There is an email address hidden in these chronicles. Tocabaga is a real location. I will reply.

My name is Jack Gunn, a.k.a. "Tocabaga Jack" and these are my chronicles.

THOMAS H. WARD

JUNE 19, 2025

It was early when Colonel Turner phoned me, "Jack I wanted to tell you that my Rangers have been pulled from Fort Desoto and we are being deployed to Atlanta. That area is a hot spot for al-Qaida and drug gangs. We'll be leaving today in a few hours."

My jaw dropped when he told me this and I was speechless, but managed to ask, "Will any men still be based here?"

"Yes don't worry I am leaving Captain Sessions in command here with fifty men. The two Bradleys and Iron Maiden will also stay here for security. Ten of the Rangers staying here will have the new TALOS battle suits. Using these suits one solider is equal to ten men in combat. Ten TALOS Warriors provide you with an equivalent of a hundred man Army."

"You mean the TALOS suits aren't a myth and are in use now?"

"Special Operations has been using them for the last year. There were some problems in the beginning but now these TALOS battle suits will

1

enable us to overpower the Federal Police Force with little loss of life to our operators and soldiers. The suits are being mass produced at a secret location.

"If you want to know more talk to Captain Sessions he is back on active duty as of today."

"Ok Colonel thank you for everything and everyone here will miss your Rangers. You are part of our family now and forever."

"Thank you Jack, I'll be in touch. Stay safe."

"Colonel Turner, stay safe. Please keep me informed using my secure Army gmail account … tocabaga.jack."

Later that day the Rangers were leaving, some were flying out but most left by truck. We walked out to the road and watched the truck convoy rumble past us. We waved goodbye and yelled, "Rangers Lead the Way."

An idea came to life in modern days as a comic book and movie called Iron Man. A man invents a suit of armor and becomes indestructible. In 2011 the Army started a program called TALOS. The Army now has the exoskeleton TALOS combat units that are used from time to time for extremely dangerous missions. These TALOS units have developed into fully armored protective suits that a soldier steps into and becomes Iron man. The only difference is the soldier cannot fly.

Using the most recent model a soldier can run at 20 miles per hour all day. They can carry heavy items like big 50 caliber machine guns and 500 rounds of ammunition at the same time. Imagine a TALOS suit with two SAW machine guns, one mounted on each arm. They pin point the target and fire by eye movement and brain waves. The most important advantage is one can walk threw a hail of bullets and not even get a scratch.

A new type of reactive armor has been developed that is more or less painted on top of light weight thin titanium alloy and beryllium metal all covered with sheets of Kevlar 10 embedded with a Boron/Silicon Carbide ceramic. The paint is a kind of plastic foam that absorbs energy and behaves like reactive armor. When it is impacted by a high kinetic energy it explodes in an outward direction.

Boron/Silicon Carbide ceramic is one of the hardest materials known to man. It has been used to make ballistic armor plates since 1986. Typically it is used in bulletproof vests as well as tank armor. Upon hitting the ceramic a bullet will shatter into pieces.

Titanium is recognized for its high strength-to-weight ratio. It is a strong metal with low density. It has a relatively high melting point (more than 3,000 °F). It is non magnetic and has low electrical and thermal conductivity. Some titanium alloys achieve tensile strengths of over 200,000 psi.

Beryllium is a hard metal. The modulus of elasticity is approximately 50% greater than steel. Beryllium is two-thirds the density of aluminum. By weight, Beryllium has six times the specific stiffness of steel and Beryllium is non-magnetic.

Reactive armor is a type of material that reacts in some way to the impact of a high kinetic projectile to reduce the damage done. The most common type is explosive reactive armor (ERA), but different types include self-limiting explosive reactive armor (SLERA), non-energetic reactive armor (NERA), and non-explosive reactive armor (NxRA). The new foam plastic paint is a combination of all of these types. If damaged in battle a new coat can be painted on top and it is combat ready in minutes.

The TALOS unit is powered by a small atomic battery pack using a new technology no one has heard of. This power system just popped out of nowhere. These little batteries have over a one year operating life and never need charging. The atomic batteries provide the energy to power the electrical - hydraulic servo systems that make movement possible and super feats of strength. Sounds pretty cool right but newer and better machines have been reported but no one has actually seen them.

I have pretty much healed from the gunshot wound to my shoulder. We posted my death on the internet to try and stop the attacks of radicals coming to collect the reward money for my head. The drones have been watching Tocabaga day and night for any intruders and everything seems to be secure now.

The Rangers have pretty much cleaned up the county of gangs, drug lords, terrorists, and other undesirable people. There are however clans of evil people roving around who will kill you for your food, guns or money. It is still a dangerous evil world.

The city of St. Petersburg, the so called Green or Safe zone, is still under Federal control. People are slowly returning to their homes only to find it burned down or destroyed. Most people have two major problems which are security and obtaining food.

I was concerned that most of the Rangers were being re-deployed. They had become our good friends and part of our Tocabaga family. I said a prayer asking God to protect them from evil.

JUNE 21, 2025

It was early in the morning. I was sitting on the patio having a cup of java when old Farmer John came over to my house and asked, "Good morning Jack. I was wondering if you can take me back to the farm to pick up some things I need."

"Sure Mr. Johnson, what do you need to pick up?"

"Well I have a bunch of seeds; corn, soy bean, green beans, and so forth that I hid over a year ago. We sure could use them here. There are some other tools we can also bring back from my farm."

"Do you think we need one or two trucks to carry everything?"

"I have ten 5 gallon pails of seeds so maybe two trucks are needed to carry the seeds and tools."

"Ok, get ready and be back here by 10 am. We need to go back any way to see if that gang left your farm like we told them too. By the way how do you like it here and how is the farming going?"

"I am happy to be here and in a few months

the farm will be doing great. Maggie is a hard worker and she has a green thumb which is important. I'll see you here at 10:00."

On June 12, 2025 we went, for the first time in years, over the Skyway Bridge to Ellenton to buy a tractor. While there we had a battle at a pig farm with Mr. Horn and his boys, killing most of them. They wanted to kidnap Maggie and use her for breeding. They were a bunch of inbred bastards. On the way back we ran into eight Federal Agents who were killed by the mob at the Ellenton mall. The Agents wanted to take away the peoples' guns. We weren't going to let that happen so we helped them out a little bit and took away the Agents guns. The people revolted and wiped out the Agents.

It was an exciting day as we found old Farmer John and saved him from a terrible life by bringing him to Tocabaga. We provide him free housing and food in exchange for his tractor and knowledge of farming.

Oh, we also ran into two men who beat up Farmer John and took his house from him. After a brief encounter in I told them to leave the house by the next day. To help them understand I was serious I cut an ear off the leader, a person named Don. I have to check if they are still there. I hope not for their sake because I hate bullies and gangs.

I contacted the drone master to see if anything was going on in Ellenton area. He advised me a drone went down there and other drones flying over that area have run into some kind of electrical interference blocking the drone camera signal and pictures. Someone or something is jamming the signal. He is not sure what is causing the problems. Similar problems have happen in the recent weeks in different areas of the county.

I advised Tommy and Ron to make two Ford pickup trucks ready. Then I called Sergeant Major Willis advising him of our trip to Ellenton and asked him to bring two Hummers for security. The trip would include SGM Willis, SFC Smith, Ron, Tommy, Jim Bo, Chris, Tony, Farmer John, and me.

I hoped this would be a fast trip in and out of the area. I guessed it would take about one hour to get there, one hour loading the trucks, and one hour to drive home. Total travel time should be about three hours.

It was 10 am and we were all waiting for Farmer John at the bridge. It's June so it is already hot, 95 degrees and muggy. John slowly walked down the road toward us, he looked beat and out of breath so I told him, "John just tell us were to go or make us a map and you can stay here."

"No I want to go … I got my own reasons. I want to put some flowers on my family graves."

Tommy handed him a bullet proof vest and said, "Put this on for your protection."

We mounted up and drove off Tocabaga to the first check point on the north side of the Skyway Bridge on Route 275. This check point had six Ranges there and we informed them of our trip plans. Driving over the bridge we arrived at the southern check point and told these Rangers that we should be back in a few hours.

At the south check point on the Skyway Bridge I asked SFC Jones, "Have you seen anything unusual in the area?"

"Nope nothing not even a car has been here in days."

A few miles after this check point Route 275 turns into Interstate 75. Going down route 75 there were no cars or trucks on the highway. Since there was no traffic we put the pedal to the metal and sped along at 55 mph.

Interstate 75 was a busy highway in the old days. The old days were just 3 years ago. This was the main route for north – south traffic on the west coast of Florida. Since the government collapsed traffic on this highway has all but stopped.

Driving on the interstate you are an easy prey for any bad guys. Some however do take the risk as evidenced by burned up rusted wrecks sitting on the side of the road. Most of them are riddled with bullet holes. It was kind of spooky looking and made you wonder what happened to the people who owned those cars.

We arrived at the Ellenton exit Route 301 and noted that there was no Deputy at the check point like last time but a Sheriff's car was there. We all wondered why no officer was present but didn't think too much about it. Turning left onto Route 301 we came to Ellenton mall area and to our surprise there were no people hanging around the road like last time. Everyone was gone; it was like a ghost town.

Last time we came here there were a few hundred people lined up along the road trying to sell whatever they could. It was like a flea market. All they wanted was some food to eat.

I commented on the radio which made a static sound, "I wonder what happen to all the people that were here last time?" No one replied.

We pulled over and I asked, "Is everyone's radio working or do you have static like I do.?" Everyone had static; the radios where not working for some reason and neither were the cell phones.

We were shocked that not a single soul was here. I thought what the hell happen to the hundred plus people that lived here? We decided to complete our mission and then come back to search the area on our return.

We were turning down the road to Farmer John's house and saw an old man walking in the middle of the road. The old person was dressed in tattered dirty clothes; he saw us and waved so we stopped next to him. Farmer John said to him, "Victor … Victor Elway is that you?"

"Yes it's me John, boy you're a sight for sore eyes."

"Victor what the heck are you doing walking around here by yourself?"

Victor looked in shock and in need of water and food. He sat down on the side of the road and put his head down between his knees. Tommy went up to him and handed him a bottle of water, "Here take a drink and relax."

Old man Victor drank the water down quickly and replied, "Thanks son. Do you have anything to eat? I haven't had anything to eat in two days."

Tommy went to the truck and pulled out a couple of oranges, peeled them, and gave them to the old man along with a piece of flat bread. Victor said, "These are good, you know I use to grow oranges in the old days."

I asked, "Victor what happen here? Where did all the people go?" Victor just sat there and didn't reply; like he was thinking what to say.

After a few minutes he answered, "The Feds came here two or three days ago with monsters and rounded everyone up taking them inside the mall somewhere. I managed to sneak away. I was going to my house to hide out until they leave."

"What do you mean monsters?"

"The Feds got monsters with them. They are big and look like monsters from the future. If you shoot them the bullets bounce off. If you fight them they shoot you or burn you up. They can shoot a spark out of their arm like a bolt of lightning. It was terrible what they did; I never seen anything like it in my whole life. I think they killed everyone, men, women, and kids.

"I saw the monsters put some bodies into empty stores at the mall and stack everyone up like cord wood."

"Where are these monsters now Victor?"

"They are somewhere around the mall. I don't know where exactly."

"How did these monsters get here?"

"I think they came by truck. For a few days I heard trucks coming in and out of the Ellenton area. I thought it was you Army guys."

"Ok, let's finish getting the seeds and tools then we can check out the monsters later. Victor get in the pickup with John." I wanted to get out of there fast!"

Pulling up to Famer Johns' house we noticed that the gang's car was still there so I said to Willis, "Shit I told these guys to leave; now they're in big trouble. Let's surround the house and flush them out."

Everyone got out of the trucks and racked a

round into their weapons. Half of us went to the back of the house and half stayed in front. Willis yelled, "US Army Rangers anyone inside come out with your hands in the air!"

No one came out, no one replied, so Willis and Smith went in the front door while we watched the back door. In a few minutes Willis shouted, "All clear in the house!"

I looked over to my left where the barn was and said, "Guys let's check out the barn." We slowly walked toward the barn pointing our weapons. Half of us went to the back and Tommy, Ron, Jim Bo and I went to the front door.

Slowly I opened the squeaking big wooden barn door with guns at the ready as I yelled, "Come out with your hands up now!" There was no reply so we pushed the door wide open and slowly stepped inside the dark dusty barn.

While searching the old barn Ron yelled out, "Here's four dead guys."

I walked over to the corner of the barn and there were four dead bodies stacked up like fire wood. One of them had an ear missing. It was Don, the guy whose ear I cut off. The bodies were full of bullet holes, a lot of bullet holes and only a machine gun could do that kind of damage. My guess was a SAW (Squad Automatic Weapon) light machine gun that did all the damage.

SGM Willis said, "I don't like this at all. Let's get the seeds and leave."

Farmer John came into the barn and lifted a trap door in the barn floor exposing the 50 pails of seeds. We proceeded to load them in the truck while John went out back behind the barn. I watched him walk up to three white crosses and place some wild flowers on the ground. I made the sign of the Cross out of respect.

We took all the tools John had in the barn, shovels, picks, a few axes, and a wood splitter. Everything was loaded up into the pickup trucks and we headed back to Ellenton area.

Someone killed the dopers for some reason, but who? I thought, good the bullies are dead and I hate bullies.

DECADES EARLIER

I have never told anyone why I hate bullies, crack heads, and gangs but it all started when I was a kid. If you have been reading my chronicles then you know how much I hate those that do not have any respect for the law. People who have no concern about how much they hurt others, they have no feelings, they just care about themselves. These people would steal from their Mother or friends without a second thought, just to satisfy their own desires.

I am the oldest of three Brothers. We grew up fighting bullies and gang members in a tough neighborhood on the south side of Chicago. My Dad one of the most honest men I have known always stressed, tell the truth, and help each other. Never ever be a bully, never steal, and try to protect those who cannot protect themselves. I have always stood up for the people who could not defend themselves. I hate liars and bullies.

When I was in sixth grade or about 12 years old I use to run home every day from school which was about a half mile from my house. I ran as fast as I could to escape the threats of a bully named Jimmy Smith. Jimmy had moved to my school about six months before and for some reason he was always picking a fight with the other kids. He was a scary looking kid with jet black hair, beady eyes, and big teeth. He had no fear of fighting but worst of all he always won the fight.

I admit that I was afraid of Jimmy as he seemed crazy. So every day I ran home because he told me he was going to beat me up to prove he is the toughest kid in the school. I told my Dad and Grandpa about the problem. My Dad told me you are going to have to fight him someday so make sure you get in some good licks by hitting him in the face a few times.

Grandpa did better than that he spent time showing me how to box as he used to be a boxer to earn extra money when he worked in the coal mines. He was a bare knuckle boxer at the age of sixteen. Grandpa started to work in the coal mines when he was 10 years old in southern Illinois. At the age of eighteen a coal car fell off the track and hit him causing him to have back injuries so he became a bull dozer driver. Grandpa never finished third grade and could hardly read a news paper.

He had a hard life growing up and was always poor. He could never afford a house and lived in a trailer for years until my Dad purchased him a house nearby after Grandpa retired. He was a tuff old guy and was not afraid of anything. Grandpa always carried a Colt 45 in his waist band. I asked him why he carried a gun and he told me just in case he needs it.

I remember looking at his huge rough hands

and large forearms from working in the mines during his teenage developmental years thinking he looked like Popeye. After a few weeks of boxing lessons and coaching from Grandpa I was ready to take on Jimmy.

Of course I had other fights with kids around the neighbor and even with my brothers, but all the kids were afraid of Jimmy. Finally I got tired of running and one day I was walking home with my brothers when Jimmy came running up hitting my brother Ron smack in the face knocking him down. That was the final straw for me so I stepped up to him and we started swinging. In two blows he was on the ground with blood gushing out of his nose and he started to cry. I told him to leave us alone and all the other kids or I would beat him up again.

This was a very important victory that molded my thinking thanks to Grandpa. Grandpa taught me don't be afraid, stand your ground, and stay calm. You need to concentrate on hitting his face and don't worry about getting hit yourself. No pain, no gain, if you worry about getting hit then you will lose the fight. Needless to say all the kids looked up to me at school and Jimmy lost is power to bully others. Maybe this is why I don't like bullies but my bully stories don't end here.

The next year I was in Jr. High School. In my seventh grade Home Room sitting next to me was the biggest fat kid in the school. His name was George

Taylor and he was a meek nice kid who minded his own business. Many kids however called George names like fat ass and he was picked on every day.

We use to have gym class and poor George couldn't do anything. He could not climb the ropes, he couldn't do one push up, he couldn't do one sit up, and he could hardly run ten feet, so basically he just sat on the side lines watching everyone else. I found out that he had some medical condition that made him over weight. He was a smart kid and I liked him because he was kind to others. If someone needed a pencil, paper, or ruler he was always the first to provide one.

One day we were in gym class and the coach told us to play flag football. Teams were selected and George was picked to be the center on my team. He would hike the ball and just stand there blocking anyone who came down the middle. One kid named Nick didn't like George blocking him. I saw Nick punching George in the arm and calling him a big fat slob. Nick was a big kid standing a head taller than me and he was a big jock that hated to lose at any game.

I went up to Nick and said, "Nick take it easy George is just doing his job blocking and if he knocked you on your ass that should teach you a lesson."

Nick commented, "Mind your own business," and punched me hard in the arm. I quickly turned throwing a right hook punching him in the gut and as *he bent over in pain I hit him with an upper cut to the jaw knocking him to the ground. He was dazed and just sat there not moving. Nick never said another word to George or me.*

Bok Lam was the only Chinese kid in our school. Bok and I became friends but he didn't have much time for playing since he worked at the family Chinese restaurant every day after school. Now you can imagine Bok took a lot of crap at school. Kids were always picking on him calling him nasty names like gook and chink. I had a number of fights sticking up for Bok as he would not protect himself.

Then after summer vacation going into ninth grade I saw Bok in gym class and he looked like Bruce Lee. All summer he studied Kung Fu gaining muscle and weight. Bok walked up to me in gym class, we shook hands, and all the other kids were looking at him because he had muscles everywhere.

Bok said to me, "Jack you don't need to protect me anymore. I will protect you from now on. I got your back." Needless to say no one picked on Bok anymore. Bok took me to Kung Fu lessons with him twice a week for the next 5 years which really improved my fighting skills. He was like a brother to me.

I was a senior in High School, my brother Ron was in 11th grade, and my little brother Mike was in 9th grade. I always wore a brown leather jacket that my

Grandpa gave me. I liked it because it cut the wind and it was warm in the winter, but the best part was it had six zipper pockets. I carried a knife, a pair of brass knuckles, a small bicycle chain, and an old .22 caliber hand gun, which I found on the street. My brother and I were always armed to the teeth and everyone knew it so not many people messed with us.

Ron and I worked in a car wash and earned enough money to buy an old 1953 Chevy for fifty bucks. We would take little Mike to school and then we would drive 10 miles to high school. Before buying the car we walked to high school threw dangerous gang infested neighborhoods. We would pack the car with a few friends like Bok and two or three others. We were a select band of brothers because I was picky about whom I called a friend. Everyone chipped in to pay for gas once a week.

Mike just turned fifteen years old and was at a local fast food place for lunch waiting in line to buy a burger. A guy came in, cut in line in front of Mike, and a fight broke out. The guy pulled out a gun and killed my little brother for a better spot in the line.

At the trial witnesses said the man cut into line and shoved Mike out of line. When Mike objected and returned the shove the crack head pulled a gun and shot Mike three times. Much to our surprise the court ruled it to be 3rd degree involuntary manslaughter and he got off with 6 years. He received six stinking years for killing my harmless little brother. Six years is not justice for cold blooded murder. This doper had a record as long as my arm for using and selling drugs. Mike was the brains of the family and he didn't get into fights like Ron and I namely because we protected him.

Six years went by and I was in the Army and received a call from Ron that Mike's killer was getting out of jail any day. I took a leave of absence when Ron confirmed he was out of jail. Ron and I plotted how to kill this guy ... an eye for an eye is my code. Up to this time I had never killed anyone but did break a lot of bones and smashed a lot of heads. I was never going to let Mike's killer get away with six years and walk around free. My Dad and Grandpa knew we were up to something but they never said a word to us.

We found out where he lived and followed him around for a week. I purchased a hot 12 gauge semi auto shot gun and a box of slugs. One night a few days later we sat in Ron's car waiting for him to come out of a local bar down town. We had purchased tickets to a movie we had already seen and made sure the manager who was a friend of ours saw us going in. We snuck out the back door. This was part of our alibi.

He came out of the bar around 11 pm drunk and staggered to his car. We followed his car and at a stop light with no other cars around, we pulled up next to him. It was summer time, his car windows were down and I yelled his name, "Leroy you piece of shit, remember me."

He looked at me and reached for a gun, as he raised it to the window his face turned white as a ghost and his jaw dropped as I pointed my big shot gun at his head from about 6 feet away. I pulled the trigger three times, hitting him directly in the head and neck. I watched his head explode into pieces. Blood and brains flew everywhere covering the inside of his windshield. He was dead on the first shot.

Then we drove away like nothing happened and went as fast as we could to our local bar. On the way we wiped off all finger prints and dumped the gun and ammo into the Chicago River. We read about his death in the paper, "Ex con Killed by Gun Fire on the Streets of Chicago." *It happens every day in Chicago.*

I chose a shot gun because slugs and pellets cannot be traced like rifles or hand guns. You just need to make sure not to leave any shells lying around. Shot guns are excellent killing weapons at close range.

Of course the cops came to our house asking if we knew anything about his death. They asked where we were last night so we told them and showed our movie tickets. The detective asked me, "Did anyone see you at the movies?"

After a long pause I replied, "Yes I think Mr. Keller the Manager saw us when we purchased tickets on the way in."

"What time did the movie end?"

"About 10:30 I think."

This was the key point because the movie theater and Bok's Tavern were both an hour away from where Leroy was killed.

"Where did you go after the movies?"

"We went to Bok's Tavern, down the street, had a few drinks and played pool."

"What time did you arrive at the Tavern?"

"I think we got there about 11 pm."

"Until what time did you play pool?"

"I can't recall exactly when we left but it was about 1 am."

"Did anyone see you at the bar?"

We had all kinds of friends who would say we were there between 11 pm and 1 am. I gave him a few names including the bar owner Bok Lam whom I could trust with my life. We were never charged with any type of crime but everyone in the neighborhood knew who killed Leroy. My Dad never said a word to us but

Grandpa told us, "Good job boys, eye for an eye." We didn't reply to Grandpa but just gave him a hug.

Funny thing is I never felt any remorse for killing that dirt bag. It actually made me feel better knowing my brother Mike could now rest in peace since justice had been served. Sometimes blind justice makes a mistake which needs to be corrected.

Anyway that's why I hate bullies and gangs.

JUNE 21, 2025

BACK TO CURRENT TIMES

Approaching the mall area on our way back to Tocabaga Victor said, "The Feds are here with the monsters. You don't want to run into them monsters."

We sat on the side of the road looking down the street for any monsters. I didn't want to get into a gun battle with the two old men along. I noticed our radios were not working correctly. They just made a static noise which seemed to be getting louder and louder. We were all standing on the side of the road except for Farmer John and Victor who were sitting in the truck.

Tommy was looking threw his .308 rifle scope trying to see off in the distance. Suddenly he said, "There it is, there's the monster about 400 yards away by that far building." Picking up the binoculars I took a look. Yes there it was and it was coming our way. It was big, very big and it was coming directly towards us.

I watched it approach step by giant step. You could hear … thump … thump with each step. It felt like the ground was shaking. I am not afraid of any man or much of anything but this huge machine scared the shit out of me. It looked scary because it was faceless and didn't look human. It had a head that was small compared to the body size. It didn't have a neck and it seemed the head was just mounted onto its huge shoulders. The monster was dark grey in color but it was almost black. The armor on it seemed to overlap, and it appeared to have some type of skin covering its body.

It was within 300 yards and started to walk faster toward us. Slowly it started to speed up and then suddenly it broke into a run, thump, thump, and thump. The thing was closing distance fast so I shouted, "Mount up let's go!" Everyone jumped in and we started to pull away as we heard gun fire and bullets zipping around us with some hitting the vehicles.

As we sped away I watched the thing, the monster running toward us at what seemed a much faster speed than a human could run. What the hell is that thing? The Humvee was too slow and it was keeping up with us at 30 mph.

I yelled to Willis, "Faster, floor it," while waving to the other trucks to speed up.

Willis was laughing and said in his best Scottish accent, "I am giving her all she got Captain Kirk. If I give her any more she's going to blow," a joke from Star Trek which I didn't see the humor in at the time.

I told Tommy, "Get on the fifty and shoot that thing."

Tommy yelled to it, "Hello Mr. Roboto, meet Mr. Fifty caliber," as he fired away. I kind of laughed at that comment mostly out of fear.

I watched as the 50 caliber machine gun hit the big monster time and time again. It finally got knocked down but stood back up, standing there as if dazed for a second or two then it started after us again. I thought this thing takes a licking and keeps on ticking.

A fifty caliber machine gun is a powerful weapon. It can shoot thru one side of a car to the other. It can blow holes in concrete walls. It takes a lot of armor to stop a .50 caliber round. The M 2 BMG or Browning Machine Gun has a muzzle velocity of 1,900 miles per hour or 2, 800 feet per second. The BMG bullet is ½ inch in diameter. I call it the Superman Bullet.

The monster was still shooting at us as we slowly pulled out of range. Looking back it was still chasing us. I looked at it again thinking this must be some kind of new TALOS suit or a robot. The robot followed us on to Route 75 and then stopped as we sped away at 55 mph.

We reached the south Skyway Bridge check point and stopped to tell the six Ranges what we had found. They laughed when I told them we saw a robot.

Our radios and phones were working now so I got on the cell phone and called Captain Sessions, "Captain, Jack here. We just ran into a new type of TALOS suit or a robot at Ellenton area. We found an old man who says these things killed everyone and stacked the bodies in the empty stores like cord wood.

"Captain this thing is big about 7 or 8 feet tall and can run at about 30 mph. Do you know anything about them?"

"No Jack, I have never heard anything about robots."

"Well I think it is still coming this way and your men here may need reinforcements."

"I think six Rangers with a 50 caliber machine gun can handle one so called robot. You head back to Tocabaga and let my men take care of it."

"Roger that Captain but our fifty rounds just bounced off this thing. I want to take some pictures of it before we return. I think this robot is jamming the radios and phones. Maybe this is why your drones are having problems."

"Ok try to get a picture then come back here but don't take any chances. Let me talk to Sergeant Dale," I handed the phone to Dale.

I told my men, "Everyone stay here while Willis, Tommy and I go back to take some pictures of the monster."

Willis was driving, Tommy was on the fifty, and I had the camera, an old Sony with 20 mega pixels with a 12x zoom lens. Tommy yelled, "There it is about 600 yards away, standing right in the middle of the road."

I replied, "This's too far away to get a good picture so drive a little closer Willis."

Tommy commented, "Any closer and we will be in firing range."

"Right that is the main idea. When it fires at us you fire back with the fifty and try to hit it in the head. Willis take us within 300 yards and make a U turn to head back. Don't slow down or stop for any reason. I want to see what this thing can do."

Willis drove up to within 300 yards then made a U turn and the monster started to fire at us. Tommy let loose with the fifty hitting the thing in the head which knocked it down but it got right back up and started to move forward toward us. It was unbelievable the fifty caliber rounds were bouncing off that thing. It was scary looking and a chill ran down my spine as I started to take pictures and video.

Willis yelled over the gun fire, "Hey we have a MK153 rocket launcher and one rocket do you want to use it?"

The MK153 SMAW means Shoulder-launched, Muti-purpose Assault Weapon. This is a hand held shoulder fired missile system used to blow up vehicles and buildings. A very powerful weapon that is reusable. You fire a missile and put in a new one.

I replied, "Good idea, let's blow this thing

up."

Willis slammed on the brakes jumped out of the Humvee while using it for cover and loaded the rocket. The robot kept coming and firing at us, it was within 100 yards and the bullets were getting to close for comfort.

Taking aim Willis fired the rocket leaving a big cloud of smoke while making a loud jet roar. I was shooting pictures and Tommy was firing the machine gun while we watched the rocket head for the target. Time slowed down like the rocket was in slow motion.

The rocket was right on target it was going to hit the monster but just before impact the robot quickly side stepped and dodged the lethal rocket like it was a toy.

I thought this thing has fast reflexes and excellent vision to dodge a rocket, we are in deep shit.

Willis jumped back in the truck and blurted out, "Did you see that the dam thing dodge the rocket!"

"I saw it Willis and got it on video, let's get the hell out of here."

Willis punched it to the floor while Tommy was still firing the big gun and soon we were out of range. I yelled over the wind noise, "We have to get these pictures back to Captain Sessions ASAP!"

Tommy said, "It stopped chasing us."

Reaching the check point we told everyone what happen. The fifty just knocked it down and it got back up. The robot dodged the MK153 rocket.

Sergeant Dale commented, "How the hell could it dodge a rocket?"

I told the Rangers, "You are going to need a Bradley or Abrams to stop that thing."

Victor commented, "There are a bunch of those monsters."

I asked him, "How many do you think?"

"I saw eight of them and maybe there are more."

"Ok Rangers good luck we have to get this information and pictures back to Captain Session, be careful."

I phoned Captain Sessions, "We got pictures of this thing. Willis fired a MK153 rocket at it to see what would happen. It just stepped aside and dodged the rocket."

"Wow that is incredible. Bring the pictures back asap."

"We are on the way now but your men here may need a Bradley here to stop these things if they come this way."

"You said things ... how many are there?"

"Victor an old man we found here told me he counted eight of them but there could be more."

"Ok see you soon, over."

Arriving back on Tocabaga John wanted Victor to move in with him. That was good as John could show Victor the ropes and the two old men could help each other. Since Victor was also a farmer he will be a great asset to help us grow more food with the new seeds.

Willis, Tommy, and I went to the Fort to give the pictures to Captain Sessions. We down loaded the camera into his computer, watched the video, and looked at the pictures. Now we were able to zoom in on the display screen and look at this monster close up.

As we looked at the pictures it was clear the armor on this machine appeared to be the same as that used on the TALOS suits. There seemed to be a small radar antenna and some other type of antennas sticking out of the head and body in various places. The head had one eye about the size of a base ball and another somewhat smaller eye.

Sessions commented, "This thing looks like a TALOS suit except for the head and the overall size of it."

Sessions saw the thing dodge the rocket on the video and commented, "It must have radar tied in with a thermal image device to be able to dodge a rocket. It also seems to sense the machine gun fire as every now and then it moves the left arm up to block bullets that would have hit it in the head.

"I am going to send this to SOCOM Intel and see what they think. They need to tell us how to kill 'em. I'll call you in the morning Jack and we can discuss these so called monsters after we get some more info."

I looked at my watch it was all ready 8 pm and I needed a drink and some food. I told Tommy and Willis, "Let's go to the bar for a drink and get some food."

Willis replied, "Sounds good to me."

"Me too," said Tommy

"See you tomorrow Captain, good night," we shook hands and left.

We arrived home around 10 pm and my wife Hemmi was happy that I was home even if I was late. The kids were all in bed and I was dead tried. We didn't say anything about the monsters to our wives. There's no need to scare them.

I had never seen anything like the robot. I knew we could be in deep shit if there was an Army of them. We could all be in the fight of our lives. We'll see what Sessions finds out tomorrow.

JUNE 22, 2025

I woke up early because I couldn't sleep. I dreamed that fire breathing monsters were invading Tocabaga and I woke up in a cold sweat. I was glad it was only a dream. I took a shower and went down for a cup of coffee. Tommy, Jim Bo, and Ron were already up. Tommy poured me a cup of mud and said, "I had nightmares last night."

I replied, "I did too, the monsters attacked Tocabaga."

We basically had the same dream. Tocabaga was in danger. I believe dreams can come true so we needed to be very careful.

The phone rang; I looked at my watch it was 6 am. Picking up the phone, "Hello, Jack here."

"Jack this is Sessions come and meet me at the Fort asap to see the Intel report."

"Ok Captain we'll be there in 30 minutes."

I told my family Sessions wants to see us now to go over the intel. Drink your coffee and let's go. We walked into Sessions office and he told us to sit down and read the Intel report.

SOCOM INTEL REPORT JUNE 22, 2025 ...
SUBJECT: ROBOTS

CLASSIFIED REPORT NO. 1223452

The pictures you sent are the first ones we have received of these robots in action. These machines have been in development over the past five years. Secretly the Federal Government has been working with the NSA (National Security Agency) to develop this new and even more dangerous combat weapon.

They are manufacturing an Army of Robots called RCCDs' or REMOTE CONTROLLED COMBAT DROIDS operated like drones by a controller or droid master sitting in a room far away from the dangers of battle field. In fact they are walking robots that have no brain, no sense of right and wrong, only that of the master controlling this monster.

They have radar, thermal imaging, and GPS systems that are the best in the world. These android soldiers along with flying drones could be a formidable force even for Army Rangers wearing TALOS suits. The only draw backs are they need to do daily maintenance and someone needs to reload their weapons when necessary.

These machines are big standing 8 feet tall at about 1000 pounds. They can carry all most any type of weapon, machine guns, rockets, and even a 25 mm cannon. They have the same armor as the TALOS units and it maybe even stronger. They can carry more weight and guns since there is no man inside. They are fast and reportedly can run at 30 mph for an undetermined distance. They don't need to eat or sleep. They are dangerous, very dangerous and offer only death to those who oppose them.

The official Army name for these androids is the "THE HEPHAESTUS ARMY" or "BOTs" for short. We warn you do not to take any chances and use maximum fire power to destroy them on sight. If you can locate the manufacturing location advise us ASAP.

END OF CLASSIFIED REPORT NO. 1223452.

After reading the report we all just looked at each other and were speechless. We were up against a very dangerous weapon that none of us had ever seen before. The question is how do we fight these things, how do we kill these things. The report didn't tell us how to kill these monsters. We need to figure out how to kill them before they come to Tocabaga.

We sat in Sessions office and looked at the pictures again. The droid had a SAW mounted on its right arm. That could be a good target because if you knock out the gun then it can't shoot. The only weak spot appeared to be if you shoot it in the head. We know it can be knocked down. What about shooting it directly in the eye, what would that do to the machine?

The only other problem is someone needs to reload the monster with ammo and do repairs as needed. We have to do a test before the "BOTs" come here. We need to shoot one in the eye to see what happens. We need to find out where are the people who are doing the reloading.

I told Captain Sessions, "Why don't Willis, Tommy and I go back to Ellenton and try to shoot one in the eye to see what happens. Tommy is the best sniper we have so let's make a plan and do it. Tommy could shoot the monster from a Hummer."

Tommy replied, "Negative, shooting this thing in the eye is a hard shot. I need to be on the ground. I can't be in a moving truck with machine guns firing at the same time I am trying to make a long distance shot. Besides that you need to get within 300 or 400 yards before it will chase you. I don't want it to even know I am out there trying to kill it."

"What about this, we go back to Route 75 where the BOT stopped chasing us. If it's not there we'll drop off Tommy in a ghillie suit on the side of the road. He digs in to cover his heat signature. When he is hidden Willis and I will go and find a BOT and get it to chase us to a kill location."

A ghillie suit is a type of camouflage clothing designed to resemble heavy foliage. Typically, it is a net or cloth garment covered in loose strips of burlap or cloth made to look like leaves and bushes. Snipers wear a ghillie suit to blend into their surroundings and conceal themselves from enemies. The suit makes the wearer's outline a three dimensional profile. A ghillie suit done correctly makes it impossible to detect the sniper.

Sessions asked, "What if the BOT detects Tommy? He could get killed. What if the BOT is still there?"

"If the BOT is still there we will set up a kill zone further down the road closer to the check point. Captain have a drone fly over there to see if the BOT is still around."

Tommy answered, "No man or any robot can find me in the bush. The critical part will be covering my body heat. I need to cover my heat signature. I'll need to use mud. A lot of mud painted all over my body and the ghillie suit. We can do a practice run here using a thermal imaging camera to find me. Do you have one Captain?"

"Yes we have a thermal imaging camera and infrared scopes we can use."

Thermal imagers are altogether different from infrared. Heat is called infrared or thermal energy. Thermal image cameras detect more than just heat; they detect tiny differences in heat as small as 0.01°C. Infrared devices only detect heat and not small differences in heat.

Everything we encounter gives off thermal energy, even ice. The hotter something is the more thermal energy it emits. This emitted thermal energy is called a "heat signature." Every item gives off a unique heat signature. It is suspected that the BOT has both infrared and thermal image capability.

"Ok let's do one test today and one tonight. I will get ready and hide at Fort Desoto within 20 feet of the roadside. When I am ready I will radio the Captain. Then have two or three men drive down the road and try to spot me."

"All right please proceed and make ready for the test in two hours."

"Roger that Captain. Dad you can help me put on the mud."

I have my own backup plan to protect Tommy in case something goes wrong. Willis and I will have two rocket systems and fire two at one time. Let's see if Mr. BOT can dodge two rockets at once. Of course my last plan is to sacrifice myself if needed to save my sons life but I hope it don't come to that.

The day and night time tests went as planned. The Rangers could not locate Tommy with the thermal or infrared device. There was only one problem which I mentioned to Tommy, "Once you fire the Cobb 50 the barrel will heat up and make a very visible heat signature."

Tommy said, "I'll wrap the barrel with fiber glass insulation and put mud on the barrel to reduce the heat. I hope it only takes one or two shots to shoot the eye."

The drone master called me, "Jack the robot is gone so it is clear right now. I had to keep the drones pretty far away from Ellenton because of the signal jamming."

"Ok thanks for the information. Please check again tomorrow at 8:00 am and let me know."

"Tommy what is your plan? The drone master just told me the BOT is gone so that means we will plant you somewhere in the bush and then we'll lure one to chase us to your specified kill zone."

"My plan is you will drop me off a about a half mile from the 301 entrance ramp. There is some high ground in that area and I will have a clear shot straight down Route 75. I will take my first shot from 500 yards away. If I don't kill it after five rounds you guys pick me up and we get the hell out of there."

"Ok good plan but if you do kill it I want to bring the thing back to Captain Sessions so we can figure out how it operates. If you miss or can't kill it then we will fire two rockets at it at the same time. Willis and Smith will handle the rockets. The BOT maybe able to dodge one rocket but not two at the same time. We'll bring a pickup truck with a trailer to carry back the body. Well it sounds like we have a good plan. Let's get a night cap and hit the hay. Tomorrow is going to be a long day."

Tommy replied, "No drinks for me tonight. I want to wake up early and do a few practice shots at 500 yards just to make sure the rifle is scoped in ok. I'll wake you at 5 am, good night."

As Tommy walked away I told the group, "This is a very dangerous mission especially for Tommy. I want to watch the video again in slow motion to see how that BOT dodged the rocket. Let's watch the whole thing in slow motion, maybe we'll see something we missed."

We went back to Captain Sessions office and watched the video again in slow motion. It seemed every time the BOT was hit in the head by the 50 caliber it stopped as if dazed just for a second or two. When it got knocked down it layed there for a second or two and got up. On getting up it seemed to be dazed trying to find the target. The BOT would turn its head right and then left, then it would look straight ahead and proceed forward. This only took two or three seconds.

Sitting there with Willis, Smith, Ron, and Jim Bo I commented, "Here is my analysis of the video. The BOT becomes dazed when hit in the head by the fifty. When it falls down and is getting back up it is still dazed. The head moves to the right and to the left. Then it looks straight ahead before proceeding. Granted it is just for a second or so but this could be a good time for Tommy to take a shot because it's not moving. I'll tell Tommy about this tomorrow.

"If you noticed this thing moved to the right when it dodged the rocket. I think it's programmed to do that or the guy operating the BOT is right handed and moves that way without thinking."

Willis asked, "So what does that mean Jack?"

"Simple, if you and Smith fire the rockets at the BOT we know it'll side step and turn to the right or we hope so. That means Willis fires first and Smith fires his rocket as soon as the first one takes off. Smith you fire just split seconds apart not at the same time."

Smith asked, "So you mean I fire just one second later?"

"Yes one second or as soon as you see it move to dodge the first rocket."

Everyone agreed it was a good back up idea in case Tommy doesn't shoot the eye out and kill the monster.

"Ok if nothing else let's get a night cap."

I thought over and over again, running our plans in my head trying to think what could go wrong. My Sons' life is on the line so I needed to be extra careful. This is probably one of the most important missions we have done.

Most of the Ranges have been redeployed so we don't have the full force of the Ranges when we need them the most. It made me wonder, why they pulled out at the same time the BOTs showed up, leaving us at a disadvantage in man power.

It seems we have a spy or someone leaking

information in order to take over Tocabaga. It would have to be someone who does not believe in freedom, limited small government, and the Constitution.

What a screwed up mess. Everyone's life on Tocabaga depends on this mission. We need to bring back a dead BOT.

JUNE 23, 2025

It was 5 am so we went to the gun range at the Fort to make sure the Cobb 50 was zeroed in and functioning correctly. While shooting I advised Tommy what was discussed last night after we watched the video and my idea about the two rockets.

I advised Tommy, "We'll Shoot the BOT in the head and knock him down. When he gets up he'll stand there for a second looking to the right, to the left, and then straight ahead before proceeding forward. That is the time to shoot him in the eye because he is not moving. This only takes a second or two."

"I agree with you Dad, that was good thinking and analysis on your part. I'll wait for him to stand up after being knocked down and then I'll blow his brains out. If he has any brains."

"Tommy these BOTs scares the shit out of me. We really need to kill one and bring the body back here for testing to find out exactly how it operates."

"Who can figure out how it operates?"

"I think the Ranger drone master is the best person to do that or send it to SOCOM."

Tommy finished target practice and we want to the shallow water to get a couple buckets of mud. Then we went home for some breakfast. It was 8 am and everyone was scheduled to meet at 10 am at the bridge.

We had three trucks, two Hummers and one F 250 Ford with a trailer to haul the body back. Jim Bo and Ron would be in the F 250. Smith and Tony were in one Humvee and Willis, Tommy and I in the other. Smith and Willis would operate the big 50 caliber guns mounted on the bullet proof Hummers and also fire the rockets if necessary.

The drone master phoned and advised no robots were on Route 75 near the Ellenton exit. So our plan was going to be hatched. We drove across the Tocabaga Bridge as our family waved good bye. The wives had no idea how dangerous this mission was or how important it was for the safety of Tocabaga. On the way out I phoned Captain Sessions telling him we were on the way. He wished us good luck.

We stopped at the Skyway Bridge north check point advising our plan on drove on to the south check point. The Rangers at this check point wanted to help us. SFC Dale jumped in my Humvee with Willis and I to operate the big 50 caliber. He assured me he was a better shot than Willis. Willis confirmed he was the best fifty gunner in the Rangers. That made me feel better as hitting this thing in the head was critical to our plan.

We reached the high ground where Tommy wanted to be dropped off. We got out and I covered him with mud. Next he put on his ghillie suit. I poured some mud on top of the suit. Not one of us said a word to each other.

Tommy picked a spot with high grass and bushes about 40 feet off the side of the road. Laying down he looked threw his rifle scope. Then he took out his laser range finder and found the 500 yard mark.

Tommy said, "Ok Dad cover me up with some bushes and put some mud on the gun barrel. The 500 yard mark is the Ellenton exit sign hanging over the highway. You try to knock the BOT down there. Be sure it is facing in my direction."

I hacked off some shrubs placing them on

top of him so no part of his body was exposed and told him, "I think you're all set. Don't take any chances. Remember when the metal man gets up he will move his head to the right and then left. Then he will look straight … shoot him then."

"Got it Dad don't worry this is a piece of cake. One shot … one kill is our motto."

"Ok good luck," I choked up a little as I walked away.

Getting back to the trucks I said, "Ron move the pickup truck about 800 yards away out of sight. Smith and Tony your position is 300 yards before the Route 301 exit sign. The exit sign is the 500 yard mark and Tommy will take his first shot there after we knock this thing down.

"When you see us speeding onto the entrance ramp the BOT will be right behind us. As soon as the BOT reaches the sign start to fire. Remember head shots only. Everyone got it?"

All replied, "Yes Sir."

I told Willis, "Let's go to the bridge and take a quick look. Maybe we can see something that would be useful."

When you exit Interstate 75 at Route 301

you make a left turn taking you under the Interstate 75 Bridge. From the top of the bridge you can see a good deal of route 301 all the way to the mall.

Willis replied, "Good idea, we can walk up on the bridge and take a peek."

We drove up to the bridge Willis and I got out while Dale waited in the truck covering us with the machine gun. Smith and Tony stopped 300 yards before the exit sign waiting there.

We looked over the guard rail on the bridge and saw robots in the road about a half a mile away. They were lining up in columns of two on route 301 as if getting ready to march somewhere. There were so many we couldn't count them all but I estimated there were at least 400 of them. We saw an estimated twenty men doing maintenance on the BOTs. They had several trucks to carry the necessary equipment and supplies.

Then looking down over the edge of the guard rail there it stood. One lone BOT standing there apparently doing guard duty. The question is can we get just one BOT to follow us or will the others also come after us. If we have a group of BOTs chasing us it would ruin our whole plan and it could ruin our whole day.

I asked Willis, "What do you think?"

"I think we are in deep shit look at all those bastards. We have to tell Captain Sessions about this."

"I agree but we need to kill a BOT and find out how they work. Here's an idea, rather than us driving down there and run the risk of being spotted by all of them, let's fire one or two shots at this one from here. When he starts coming we'll jump in the truck."

"Sounds good to me, let's do it."

Willis taking aim with his M 4 fired one shot hitting the BOT in the head. It looked in our direction but didn't move. Maybe it didn't see us so he fired one more round. This time when it looked in our direction we stood up and waved at it. That got its attention and the monster started moving toward our location.

Willis and I were laughing as we ran back to the Humvee and Dale asked, "What the heck you guys laughing at?"

Willis said, "We just shot a BOT in the head and waved to it. It seemed funny when we did it."

"It isn't funny because here it comes now."

I started the motor, Willis jumped in, and we headed for the other Humvee. The BOT like a good little dog, was following us and gaining speed. Willis fired another M 4 round hitting it in the head but the bullet just bounced off.

We reached the 300 yard spot and both trucks opened fire with the 50 caliber machine guns as it went under the exit sign. I was thinking I hope the other BOTs don't hear the gun fire.

All of a sudden after twenty or thirty rounds the BOT fell down and we stopped firing. It got up moved its head to the right, then to the left, and then straight. We could hear the bullet whiz by us as it smashed into the baseball sized eye. Tommy made a direct hit on the first shot.

The BOT fell down on its back and began shooting into the air. The robot's legs and arms where flailing around. It was still alive but couldn't stand up. It was flopping around like a fish out of water. It was clear the eye was a camera and also had something to do with the gyroscope that enabled this thing to walk and keep its balance.

A gyroscope is a device for maintaining orientation. There are many types of Gyroscopes such as the electronic, microchip-packaged MEMS found in consumer electronic devices, fiber optic and the extremely sensitive quantum gyroscopes.

Willis commented, "Shit what do we do now?

"Smith tell Ron to bring up the trailer. We need to get some rope or cable and tie this thing's arms and legs. Anyone have any rope?"

Willis had about 50 feet of half inch rope in the Hummer, picking it up we walked over to the BOT who had now ran out of ammo. As Willis, Dale, and I approached it we stood near the big round head and saw the eye was gone. It still had one more eye but we didn't know what that was for. We made it a point to stay away from its left arm which contained a taser like device.

To our surprise the robot started to speak in a deep metallic voice, "YOU ARE UNDER ARREST FOR SHOOTING A FEDERAL OFFICER; DROP YOUR WEAPONS NOW. BACK UP IS ON THE WAY. RESISTANCE IS FUTILE." That scared the crap out of us so we both jumped back.

I instantly unloaded a full mag. of 20 rounds into its eye hole. It still kept moving like it was in pain and was still repeating the same words over and over.

I said, "This dam thing is creepy."

Willis pulling out his .357 magnum hand gun and said, "Die fucker," as he aimed the revolver at the other eye and fired. The bullet bounced off the eye leaving a slight mark. It finally stopped moving but the BOT was still talking.

Willis said, "Cut off the antennas, there's a wire cutter in the Hummer under the back seat."

I ran to the truck and pulled out the big wire cutters. I cut off four antennas and the robot stopped talking. Ron and Jim pulled up with the trailer. We were standing there looking at it and SFC Dale yelled here they come. Then he opened up with fifty caliber machine gun. We all turned around and saw ten BOTs moving our direction.

I yelled, "Pick this thing up and put it on the trailer so we can get the hell out of here!" Six of us could barely lift it but we managed to drop it on the trailer. We didn't have any time to tie it down.

I shouted to Ron and Jim as they took off

with the captured dead BOT, "Pick up Tommy!"

Willis and I ran to our Humvee. Dale was firing at the droids knocking some of them down. Then we heard a bullet zip by, it was Tommy shooting and he knocked down another BOT hitting it in the eye. Another bullet zipped by and one more BOT hit the ground.

We were a good distance away when the robots stopped shooting at us, then I heard a loud explosion and Willis yelled, "A rocket just hit Smith's Humvee. The robot fired a rocket!"

I slammed on the brakes and backed up about 50 feet to the burning truck. Tony and Smith were trapped inside. It was on fire and the rear end was destroyed. Willis and I pulled Tony and Smith out of the burning wreck. Tony was severely injured and had been knocked out from the explosion. Smith was on fire and his clothes were in flames. Willis put out the flames and tore off his clothes. Then we loaded Tony into the back of the Humvee.

Smith was standing in the road almost naked with burns over most of his body and yelled, "Be sure to get the rocket!"

Willis replied, "I got it."

A naked wounded Smith screamed, "Let's blow these bastards up!"

It was a perfect set up the droids where standing almost in a straight line. If we fire a rocket and one manages to dodge the rocket, it will hit the BOT behind it. Willis and Smith picked up the rocket launchers.

Taking aim Willis yelled, "Missile one away," as he fired.

Smith replied, "Missile two away."

We all watched the missiles fly to the targets, the first robot in line saw the missile and side stepped to the right but the second and third robots in line didn't see them in time ... KABOOM ... KABOOM. Two robots were down which proves we can blow them up. They fell to the ground in a heap of twisted smoking metal.

Smith yelled, "Take them bastards to the junk yard!" Then he fell to the ground and passed out. He was in bad shape so we loaded him into our Hummer and covered him with a blanket.

Dale was still firing the fifty the whole time and he shouted, "I killed one, shot him right in the eye!" We had killed six BOTs proving that these things, these monsters are not invincible. We had a robot to take back for analysis which would help us figure our other methods to defeat them.

We sped away leaving behind the blown up smoking Humvee. The remaining four robots stopped at the wreckage and seemed to be checking if any people were inside.

Reaching the south check point we told the Rangers what had happen. They advised us that Ron had just left with the BOT on a trailer. He stopped long enough for the Rangers to see it. We told them how to kill the dam things.

I got on the radio to Ron asking, "Bro did you pickup Tommy?"

"No we thought you were going to pick him up."

"Shit I told you to pick him up."

"I couldn't hear you over all the noise and gun fire."

I didn't say another word to Ron and told Willis, "Tommy was left behind. We have to go back and find him. I think he is near the spot where the Hummer got hit by the rocket, right around where the BOTs stopped."

Willis asked a Ranger at the check point to take our truck and rush Smith and Tony back to Tocabaga for medical attention. He didn't want to risk unloading Tony which could cause more damage if he had back injuries. Tony was still unconscious and he was bleeding from his wounds. There was no way to tell how serious he was wounded. Smith was now going into shock from his burns. He was shaking like crazy so I put another blanket over him.

Willis, Dale, and I borrowed a Humvee from the check point and headed back to find Tommy. As we approached, about 800 yards away, we could see the burning truck in the road and two BOTs were standing near to it. The other two were near the side of the road very close to Tommy's sniper nest. They seemed to be scanning the area walking back and forth, stopping, scanning, turning their heads, they were looking for Tommy.

It appears that the robots can't see us at 800 yards. Thinking back at the first contact we had the other day the robot didn't start to chase us until it was within 400 yards. They didn't fire at us until they were within 300 yards, if I recall correctly.

The problem now is we have to draw these robots away and still be able to rescue Tommy. We needed a plan right away so I asked Willis, "You got any ideas how we can draw them away from Tommy?"

"This sounds stupid but it may work. We drive right up to within 300 yards and Dale starts shooting each one in the head to get their attention. We speed by them and let them chase us back to the 301 exit. That will draw them away from Tommy."

Dale commented, "You mean go back to robot town? We could get trapped."

"Maybe, maybe not, we may have to shoot our way out … but my idea is to get off at the exit and go around under the bridge and get right back on Interstate 75. Then we race back and pickup Tommy. Maybe the BOTs aren't that smart and won't understand what we are doing. Maybe they will follow us."

We all just sat there for a few minutes … our brains computing what Willis just told us. What are the chances of this working? What are the chances of this working without any of us getting killed?

Dale pointing down the road toward the BOTs said, "We better do something soon one robot is moving off the highway into the bushes very close to the sniper location."

Without further thinking I ordered, "Let's go kill some more robots.

"Willis do we still have any rockets?"

"Yes we have two, what do you want to do?"

"Here is the plan, I'll drive, Dale on the fifty, Willis on the rocket. We will speed right by them firing the fifty the whole time. I'll stop when we are about 400 yards past of them. When they begin to chase us Dale you try to knock one down and when he gets up, Willis will blow it up. I think it'll work. Dale maybe you'll get lucky and hit one in the eye again."

Dale already proved the M2 machine gun could kill a BOT but the problem was aiming the dam thing. Once the fifty starts to rock and roll it is hard to control and precise targeting is all but impossible. Yes it is possible if you fire enough rounds you might get lucky and hit one in the eye.

Dale and Willis both agreed and I said, "Rangers Lead the Way," they repeated the motto.

Into the face of death we drove, no fear, just

determination to finish the mission and rescue a fellow warrior. No one ever gets left behind, dead or alive, that is the Ranger creed.

All of a sudden it hit me, how could the robot find Tommy? I looked at Dale and then at Willis they all had one thing in common the electronic dog tags. I told both, "I think these droids can track your dog tag signal. That's why they are looking for Tommy. Give me your tags and we'll drop them on the side of road when we make the U turn under the bridge. That just might confuse them."

Dale said, "That sounds like a good idea."

I floored the Hummer and we were quickly approaching the robots so Dale started to fire. The droids watched us go past them and stop. Dale got their attention as 50 caliber rounds were hitting them in the head. Willis was ready to fire the rocket. The four BOTs were now coming towards us and finally Dale knocked one down at about 200 yards away. The other three started to fire at us.

I was looking to see if the robots had anymore rockets, and I didn't see any, thank God. The knocked down metal man was getting up; Willis fired the rocket just as it stood up and …

KABOOM, it was blown to shit. One more piece of junk was down.

I punched the pedal to the metal and speeding up to 35 mph just enough to stay ahead of the three stooges following us. Bullets were hitting our vehicle but had no affect due to the armor plating. The stooges were now about 200 yards behind us as we approached the 301 exit.

Driving down the exit ramp and making a left turn Willis yelled, "Shit more robots." Standing in the road, under the bridge, three BOTs were blocking our way.

I yelled, "Dale shoot these guys. I am going to run them over!"

Willis replied, "Go for it." I wasn't sure what was going to happen but hitting a 1000 pound object at 35 mph was not a good idea. We had no choice but run them over or die trying.

I hit the gas and yelled, "Hold on tight," as we slammed into the first BOT hitting him in the lower legs and he flew over the top of the truck. It jarred the hell out of us but the Army Hummer kept going. BAM another bone jarring hit and this one tumbled to the side of the road. The third BOT moved out of the way. Going under the bridge I threw the dog tags out of the window as far as I could.

We ran over two BOTs and I could tell that the left front tire was flat. Humvee's have run flat tires but you can feel the difference with no air in tire. Steam started to come out of the radiator as we went up the interstate entrance ramp. The tin men were shooting everything they had at us; the bullets were hammering the back of the truck.

Dale started shooting again and he advised us, "The robots are going after the dog tags … most of them stopped chasing us."

My foot was on the floor and our top speed was only 45 mph but we were pulling away from the tin men. Slowly but surely we reached the location Tommy was at located about one hundred yards from the still smoking Humvee.

I yelled, "Tommy we're here!" There was no reply and to make matters worse our truck engine stopped running. I tried to restart it but the motor just turned over, it had over heated, it was dead.

"Well guys Tommy isn't here. He must have escaped somehow."

I tried to raise the hood to check out the motor but the front end was smashed in from hitting the tin men and I couldn't open it.

I commented, "The truck is done for we better start humping it back. We have about 15 miles back to the check point."

Willis said, "Hey try the cell phone."

I pulled mine out but it wasn't picking up a signal. I tried the radio and heard static. I told Willis, "They're not working."

Dale was just sitting in the truck gun turret not moving and Willis said, "Hey shit head does your phone work?" Dale didn't reply.

Willis and I climbed into the truck and we saw red blood running down Dale's arm. Dale was slumped over the machine gun. He had been shot in the neck. Willis felt for a pulse but there was none, he was dead. He must have bled out not knowing he was seriously wounded.

Willis laid his friend down in the back of the truck and we put him in a body bag. Willis said, "We'll be back for you my friend. No one gets left behind.

"He was a great solider, a good man, a great

person, and good friend."

We both bowed our heads and said the Lord's Prayer.

I said, "Willis I don't think there was anything we could have done to save his life the bullet it his juggler vein. We'll come back for him ASAP."

We started jogging down Interstate 75 to the check point fifteen miles away. We had jogged about 3 miles and we stopped for a break to try the phone or radio. They were still not working. While sitting there I heard the faint sound of a motor and looked in the sky for a drone.

I yelled look, while pointing in the air, "There's a drone."

Willis said, "That's not our drone, we don't use that model."

I put my ear to the ground, on the cement roadway, I could hear … THUMP … THUMP … THUMP, and the sound sent a chill down my spine. I told Willis, "They're coming."

Willis asked, "How far away do you think they are?"

"It's hard to tell but I would guess about five miles behind us. That little drone gave away our location. Let's shoot it down." Willis and I both started shooting at the drone. One of us hit it and it tumbled from the sky.

"Jack let's double time it to the check point."

"I agree." We started to run at a fast trot. About an hour later I was huffing and puffing.

I looked at my watch, the sun was going down, and it was already 8 pm. While gasping for air I told Willis, "We're not going to make it ... to the check point before dark. Let's hide ... under the bridge ... up ahead where ... 275 crosses 75. The concrete ... and steel will help us ... by blocking our heat signature."

Willis just nodded and replied, "It's about two more miles from here can you make it?"

I just nodded yes, because I was so out of breath.

Interstate 75 splits off into 275 which goes to St. Petersburg. Then 75 continues on to Tampa. Interstate 275 curves up and over 75 so there is a bridge there. If we hide out under the bridge the concrete and steel would provide us some cover from the all seeing metal men and the drones.

By the time we arrived at the bridge it was dark and we both crawled up under the bridge to hide our heat signature from the thermal scanners. We crawled up deep inside where the steel beams and the concrete road meet. We fell down exhausted and took a drink from our camel backs.

I asked Willis, "How much ammo do you have left?"

"Not that it matters since these guns do nothing to the robots but I have 6 mags."

"I have six also and three mags of 9 mm."

We laid there catching our breath and we could hear another drone flying over head. All was quiet except for the drone buzzing around searching for us. Then we heard THUMP and the THUMPING was becoming louder by the minute.

Within thirty minutes they were right on top of us walking on the bridge we were hiding under. The whole bridge was shaking when all of a sudden the marching stopped. The thumping stopped and Willis not saying a word signaled me he was going to take a peek. I was thinking that's not a good idea.

Willis went to one end and I watched him pop up and do a fast, very fast look. He crawled back next to me and whispered, "They're here. It looks like there's a shit load of them."

The robots have closed in on us. Willis and I looked at each other and shook hands without saying a word. We both knew this could be the end and we would fight these bastards to the death.

We kept waiting for a BOT to come under the bridge. Funny as it seems the metal heads were not smart enough to look under the bridge. They had no idea we were sitting right below them. Maybe we can try and get some rest. One man sleeps while the other watches in two hour shifts. Willis was first to rest because my adrenalin was too high. I laid there looking and listening for anything.

It was dark, very dark because there was no moon. I could here men talking and trucks running above us. They were doing the necessary maintenance to the walking death machines.

I hoped and prayed Tommy made it back ok. I

also wondered why Ron had not returned for us with reinforcements. Using logic I guessed they would wait until daylight to come after us.

We only needed to hold out until then, but if the metal men come for us I don't know what we're going to do. We need to make a plan. I can't sleep with danger standing right over my head.

JUNE 24, 2025

I let Willis rest longer than two hours. I looked at my watch it was 3 am and dark as shit. It had started to rain. I was trying to think of a plan to escape in the dark. Now was the time to make a move as the robot handlers' were probably sleeping, except for a few on guard duty.

Then I heard a noise, not a loud noise but so soft I could barely hear it. I woke Willis up whispering, "I think we got company."

It could be an animal of some kind, it could be a person, or it could be a BOT. Willis and I laid there looking into the dark, down at the foot of the bridge where the noise was coming from. It sounded like bushes moving but due to the sound of the wind and rain falling I couldn't tell.

Then I saw what looked like some kind of animal crawling on the ground. It was fairly large in size, as big as a human. I couldn't make out the shape of it in the dark. Maybe it was a Black Bear. There are a lot of bears around here because no one hunts them. Back in the old days 270 bears were killed in one year from cars hitting them while crossing the road at night. Night time is when bears hunt.

I thought great, if we shoot this bear then the metal men will wake up and if we don't kill it then we could be killed.

I looked at Willis he pulled out his small 4 inch knife and we sat there watching this thing moving towards us slowly but surely. I said to Willis, "That's not a knife, this is a knife." I pulled out my 8 inch double edge Cold Steel Black Bear fighting knife, thinking how ironic using a Black Bear knife to kill a bear. It was twenty feet away when I recognized what it was.

It was Tommy in his ghillie suit; he stood up and softly said, "Hi guys what's up?"

I wanted to give him a big hug but I replied, "We were waiting for you. Did you think you could sneak up on us?" I didn't want him to know I was worried. Man I was relieved and happy to see him, so happy I think a tear dropped from my eye.

I asked him, "How did you get away from the BOTs?"

"Those BOTs are dumb and they don't see too well. I saw Uncle Ron drive by me then I knew someone fucked up and forgot about me. You stopped about 100 yards from me when the Hummer got blown up. I saw you take off with Tony and Smith but I stayed hidden to provide cover fire in case they shot a rocket into your Humvee.

"The robots came up the side of the road looking around the blown up Hummer. I couldn't understand how come they were searching near me. Then I realized maybe it was the electronic dog tag. So I took it off and threw it as far away from me as I could."

"We thought the same thing; they can track the dog tags so we threw them away," Willis commented.

"While they were looking for the tag I slowly crawled away a few inches at a time. Anyway I escaped but it wasn't easy. I saw you come back for me but I was about a mile away in the swamp."

The reason Willis and I stayed on the road was because it was the safest place to be. To get back to check point on the Skyway Bridge there is a river to cross and each side of the road is a swamp making it almost impossible to walk. Hiking through the dense under grow in the swamp is almost impossible. Swamps are also full of snakes and other nasty critters like gators.

Tommy asked, "Hey where is Dale?"

Willis told Tommy, "Dale was killed he took a round in the neck. His body is still in the Hummer. Tony and Smith were both wounded and burned. Hopefully they are receiving medical treatment by now."

Tommy said, "Shit, Dale got killed coming back for me. Dam I don't know what to say."

We all sat there speechless for a minute as no one knew what to say, then Tommy asked, "So what's the plan to get out of here?"

I told him, "We don't have a plan. You got any ideas?"

"Yep, let's make some mud and we'll crawl out of here the way I came in."

"By the way what made you come here under the bridge? Were you looking for us?"

"I saw you both from the swamp and I

guessed you would hide under the bridge since you couldn't out run the robots. I didn't count on them stopping right on top of the bridge."

"We didn't count on that either. I feel better seeing you with the Cobb 50 at least we have something to kill them with."

"Negative the Cobb has a broken trigger return spring. I could have killed more BOTs if the spring didn't break. Ok let's make some mud because we need to leave before it gets light. I hope it keeps raining cause that will help us sneak away."

While making the mud I asked Tommy, "Give us some intel, what do you know about these things?"

"Well there are about 100 of them above us. There are 50 men who do the reloading and daily repairs. They follow behind the army with ten panel trucks and two big semi trailers.

"One important thing I discovered is they can't see what is behind them. However, they do have some kind of radar that will pick up movement behind them. If the radar picks you up they will turn around. I don't know how sensitive the radar is but it didn't pick me up when I was slowly crawling away from them on the ground.

"The guys who fix them all have some kind of an ID card hanging around their necks on a chain. I think this is similar to our electronic dog tags. It gives a signal to the robot that this man is ok. They walk up behind the BOT and slide the card into a slot in the upper back, like swiping a credit card. I assume that disables the thing. When they are done working on it they swipe the card again. Oh, I almost forgot the work men don't carry any type of weapon."

Willis commented, "That is pretty important information if you ask me. Tommy do you think the BOTs are remote controlled like the drones are?"

"Yes I do, put it this way they are receiving a satellite signal. If we could jam the signal we could stop the BOTs in their tracks. The droid controller can see using the BOT eye camera and moves them around probably by use of a joy stick. They could be anywhere in the US. I assume each robot has one man controlling it."

"Why do you think the robots are coming all the way to Route 275?"

"I don't think they are here just to find you

guys. I think they are going to Tocabaga. Remember they are the FPF (Federal Police Force). We already kicked their ass once, killing a lot of them. We took the FBI and AFT cars and the agents were killed by the mob at Ellenton. The FPF has a score to settle."

I told Tommy, "I agree they are coming to Tocabaga sooner or later. Based on your information it would be great to get one of their ID cards. Maybe capture one of the work men. How good is their security?"

"The men and trucks are probably guarded by the robots 24-7 making it very difficult to get near them but not impossible. Remember we don't have a truck to help us get away."

I told Willis and Tommy, "I wish we could nab a man, take his card, ask him some questions, and then kill him on the spot. We can't let him go and I don't want to take him to Tocabaga so we have no choice but to kill him."

Suddenly Tommy held up his hand putting his finger to his mouth and softly said, "Someone is coming." I didn't hear a dam thing but saw the outline of a man approaching in the dark walking under the bridge out of the rain.

I got my wish a man walked under the bridge, pulled down his zipper and took a leak. Then he stood there about fifty feet away watching the rain, pulled out a pack of smokes and lit up a butt. He didn't see us or even look around in our direction but we saw him. He was a short pudgy guy whom I guessed was about 240 pounds and around 5 foot 6 inches tall. Since he didn't have a gun, according to Tommy, it was our chance to nab one of these jerks.

I whispered to Tommy and Willis, "Watch this."

I softly walked down from deep under the bridge on this moonless rainy night getting closer and closer to him. He heard me when I was about 15 feet away. He turned and quickly glanced at me in the darkness and I said, "Hey friend you got an extra smoke?"

"Yes I do. What are you doing up so late?"

He reached in his pocket to pull out a smoke without looking at me as I drew my knife out. I was now standing right next to him as he turned to hand me a smoke. Seeing me close up he said, "Hey, you're not one of us!"

I replied, "No shit stupid ass," while

thrusting my 8 inch knife blade to his throat.

He still handed me a smoke and even gave me a light. I took a deep drag and blew smoke in his face while saying, "Thanks don't try anything stupid like yelling, or I'll cut your throat." I held the knife against his neck and knew if I put just one more pound of pressure on the blade it would draw blood.

"Move up here under the bridge," giving him a push in the right direction.

He answered, "Ok I'll do whatever you want, just don't kill me."

I think he was scared to death seeing the three of us with faces covered in mud. I pushed him down between me and Tommy. He had on a nice black uniform with a matching hat. He looked like a weak little geek wearing black rimmed glasses that had white tape holding them together in the middle. He appeared to be about fifty years old.

Tommy told him, "Give me your card and tell us how it works."

Taking the card off his neck and handing it to Tommy he asked, "Are you the guys damaging our RCCD units?"

Willis replied, "If you mean robots, we're the ones killing them."

He stuck out his fat little hand to me saying with a smile, "Hi my name is Dr. Carl Urban." I didn't shake his hand and looked at him like he was nuts.

I asked, "Doctor of what?"

"I have a PhD in Robotics from USF (University of Southern Florida) and I invented the RCCDs or Remote Controlled Combat Droids. It's your lucky day finding me because I want to help you."

"Why do you want to help us?"

"I have several good reasons. I first had the idea to make an RCCD from the movie "The Day the Earth Stood Still" an old film from 1951. A space ship came to earth and had a robot named Gort. Gort was a humanoid shaped robot and he was a police officer. His job was to end crime and keep the peace. He fired a laser beam out of his one eye which would vaporize anything. He had a type of skin that covered his whole body. Bullets or rockets would just bounce off of him and he was big standing at eight feet tall.

"The RCCD Units were supposed to be used for crowd control, riots, or to combat gangs, terrorists, and general police work when it was too dangerous for human officers. The FPF decided to use them as an Army. I told them that wasn't a good idea, but they didn't listen to me.

"The FPF decided to test them and brought them to Ellenton to control the population which they claimed killed eight Federal agents. I was horrified at what they did. The RCCD units killed almost every person at Ellenton. They put the bodies in the empty stores stacking them up like they were just some garbage. My guess is 300 people were murdered and anyone who had a gun was killed for sure.

"I didn't intend for the Units to be used like this. I wanted them to be used for good, to help people and make society better. I was brained washed into thinking the Federal Government was doing something worthwhile. Then the President declared Executive Order 13603 taking away all our rights and that is when I knew the truth. Power corrupts and absolute power corrupts absolutely, so no one is safe. When Hitler was in power he slowly took full control of the German Government and Army, just like what is happening now."

Tommy advised the little guy, "Now you know the government lies."

Dr. Urban stated, "You guys are pretty smart figuring out how to defeat my RCCD units. You know no one has ever destroyed one before. The FPF did five tests trying to defeat the Units and each one failed. Tell me how did you capture the one Unit?"

This little fat man would not shut up. He acted like we were his long lost friends. Finally I said, "We just shot one of his eyes out. Now tell us how these things work," while pressing my knife against his neck.

The little nerd asked, "How did you shoot the eye out because it is bullet proof?"

"We used a Cobb 50 rifle."

"I knew the camera eye was a weak spot."

Tommy asked again, "What about the card, how does it work?" Tommy passed the card over to me to check it out.

"Ok I'll tell you but first I want you to know that I am really on your side."

"Well you're going to have to prove that,"

Tommy replied.

"All right ... the security ID card has several functions. It sends a radio signal to the Unit, actually to all the Units that you are a friend. It is used to deactivate the Units. Every man carries the same card. To deactivate a Unit there is a slot in its back and you just insert the card and pull it back out. It's like using a credit card. The Unit is then disabled and one can work on it safely. To reactivate a Unit you just swipe the card again."

"Ok tell us more."

"The Units are programmed to detect any type of weapon. If it senses a weapon then you become a target. If you shoot at it or are hostile in any manner it will take action to neutralize the threat.

"One problem is the Unit is controlled by a human. Each Unit has an operator or Master that controls the Units actions. It is similar to how a drone works. There is a man watching on a computer screen thru the RCCD eyes. He controls how the RCCD moves and so forth, including when to fire the weapon systems. It is like playing a video game. The Units are still subject to human error."

He was smiling all the time while telling us this information and was giving me the creeps. I was thinking this guy created the Frankenstein Monster. I asked him, "Tell us more about the weapon systems and what do all those antennas do?"

"All Units carry a SAW machine gun and 1000 rounds of ammunition and all Units can fire from the left hand a … for lack of a better word … a taser, but it's more like a lightning bolt. It can terminate a human if fired for more than five seconds. A person will just burn up. It has a range of 20 feet putting out 20 million volts at 20 amps. They have metal hands with a big thumb and no single fingers. The fingers are all one piece so the hand looks like a mitten. It can pick things up and even cut off an arm if it grabs you."

I commented, "Shit that is why Victor told us that people were burned up."

"Yes that is what really made me upset and turned me against the Feds. That was the last straw for me. The antennas are for radar, GPS, signal jamming, and card detection."

"Tell us about the signal jamming," I commented.

"Each Unit can jam any type of signal, cell phone, radio, or radar. The range of one Unit is less than a half mile. As more Units come within 300 feet of each other the more powerful the jamming capability becomes. One hundred RCCDs can jam signals up to 20 miles away.

"Ok what else can you tell us?"

"We have 20 Units that are modified to shoot a rocket. It is basically the same hand held rocket used by the military but is aimed by a laser beam. The Unit aims the beam and the rocket goes to the target. They only carry one rocket at a time, mounted on the left arm."

Willis asked, "How many Bots do you have here and how many total are there?"

"Here on the bridge we have 100 Units. There is another 300 back at Ellenton and the FPF have a grand total of almost two thousand deployed in different states. Currently there are ten Units being produced per day at a secret lab at the USF technology campus in St. Petersburg, Florida which is paid for by the Government. They are being produced in a building that was the old Dali Art Museum.

"Where are the Masters located," Willis

asked.

"Oh, the controllers are located in Washington DC inside a bunker near the White House. The plan is to make a large Army of 100,000 to keep the Military under control. That won't work however because they will need 100,000 controllers. Can you imagine trying to organize the controllers into a fighting army? The Units will be running into each other on the battle field."

Willis told Carl, "I could see that happening. By the way how are the Units constructed? What types of materials are used?"

"The RCCD Unit bodies are made using the same methods as the Army TALOS suits. Somehow the FPF managed to steal the material plans for the TALOS suits. Other than that they are completely different on the inside. The Units are much more complicated.

"RCCDs have radar, GPS, thermal sensors, infrared, and a very sensitive gyro device that allows them to walk and run. When you shoot one in the head enough times it throws the gyroscope out of balance for a few seconds."

I pressed him for more information, "Ok

Carl what else can you tell us?"

"I can't tell you much more but I can be of more help."

"How can you help us?"

"Well first tell me your names, since we are kind of friends now."

"I wouldn't say we're friends yet Carl, but my name is Jack Gunn, this is Army Ranger Sergeant Major Willis and that's Tommy in the ghillie suit."

"You're ... Jack Gunn ... on the internet it shows a picture of you dead, killed by al- Qaida terrorists. The article stated that you have killed more than a few people."

"Yep I'm Jack Gunn and yes al-Qaida did try to kill me twice but I am still here. I've killed people but only those who deserved it or needed killing."

Sticking out his hand again, "Mr. Gunn it is a pleasure to meet you. I want to become one of your group. I don't like al-Qaida or any terrorist organization."

I again ignored his hand shake offer.

Willis said, "Jack he could be a real asset to the Army when it comes to fighting these robots. He could help us to jam their signals."

Scratching my unshaven mud covered face I asked, "Tommy what do you think?"

"Yes he could be of help if we can trust him."

Carl answered, "After all I told you guys and you still don't trust me. Ok here is the offer. One of those semi trucks is assigned to me and me alone. Inside of the truck are ten Units along with the ability to control them. I will teach you how to use them and help you jam the FPF RCCDs. I have the newest state of the art Units."

Willis said to me, "That does it Jack. Carl is now working for the Army Rangers. We have to take him and that truck back to the Fort."

I responded, "Carl how are you going to steal that truck?"

"Easy, I'll just walk up get inside and drive away."

"No one will stop you? What about the robots they won't stop you?"

"I have a master switch that turns off all the Units sensors, so they can't see anything. It turns off the camera, radar, and everything. As for the men they don't question what I do since I am the boss.

"There are two Guard Units that cannot be turned off. These are real robots that think and reason on their own. Their job is to provide security for the technicians. They won't pay any attention to me."

"I have one more question, what were you going to do with these 100 Units? Where were you going?"

"Originally we came to Ellenton for a trial run. We were doing recon for the main force which will go to Tocabaga. The FPF wants Tocabaga for a base of operations."

"Carl, do you know we live on Tocabaga."

"I guessed that you did. So I want to go with you. I am on your side now."

Tommy told Carl, "Ok go get your truck and I'll cover you from here. If you try to warn anyone make no mistake I will kill you."

"Don't worry about that Tommy. My truck

is the very first one just give me about 10 minutes and I will pick you up. I need to turn off the Units' sensors and lock the trailer doors."

I asked, "When you turn off the sensors how long will that last?"

"Good question Jack. It all depends how long it will take the other technicians to figure out what I did. I think it will take them two or three weeks and maybe months. No one knows I made a master switch in case things got out of control."

"What about the other 300 BOTs back at Ellenton are their sensors turned off also?"

"Yes, no unit will be able to function."

Willis commented, "That sounds great to me. It gives us some time to make a battle plan. Go get the truck Carl."

Tommy watched him walk up to the truck and said, "I believe him he wants to be one our side."

Willis and I both agreed. It was a good thing I didn't kill him. I kind of like this little nerd.

We heard the truck engine start and saw the head lights come on lighting up the dark rainy night. We stood on the side of the road just under the bridge as Carl pulled up and stopped next to us. As we jumped inside of the truck cab we were shocked to see another man inside driving and Carl was sitting next to him.

Willis pointing his gun at the man's head asked Carl, "Who the hell is this?"

"He's ok Willis, please put down your gun. This is my technical aid and driver. His name is Dr. Alvin Sinclair." Alvin gunned the motor and the big truck leaped forward throwing us all off balance into the back of the cab.

Willis commented, "You didn't tell us there would be another man."

"No I didn't because you guys would want to ask him a lot of questions and we need to get out of here before daylight. Alvin and I have been friends for twenty years. I trust him with my life and so should you. He helped me develop the Units. He does all the actual work … nut and bolt turning and so forth and I am the brains."

I told both of them, "You guys need to earn trust. Go down 75 until the first U turn. Turn around and go back to the 275 and get on ramp to St. Petersburg."

Alvin replied, "Yes Sir, that is what I was going to do."

Alvin was a little skinny bald headed nerd who had on big thick glasses. He was probably 120 pounds soak and wet. He had on the same nice black uniform. He just looked like a sneaky little freak with his long hooked nose and big ears. I wasn't happy we had another robot nerd with us. It made me uneasy and I have a feeling their background checks will prove them both to be socialists or communists.

Dr. Alvin drove the semi up to the Ranger check point and I told him to stop 50 feet away. It was just turning daylight as Willis and I got out telling the Rangers what we were doing. We advised them that there were 100 BOTs about 5 miles away that had been disabled. Willis advised them to obtain some extra rockets and have a Bradley brought up to the check point for extra security.

We drove away going over the Skyway Bridge and I got on the speaker cell phone to Captain Sessions, "Captain we captured a truck load of ten BOTs and two guys' who invented them. We're headed back to Tocabaga now and we'll be there in 30 minutes. It's been one hell of a night."

"Good work Jack, I don't know how the heck you managed to do that but bring the truck directly to the Fort and park near the Helo area. I'll be waiting there with a security team.

"Ron told us you were in trouble and we were going to send a rescue team after you today. Who are the two men you captured?"

"The head honcho is Dr. Carl Urban and the other is Dr. Alvin Sinclair, his assistant.

"Captain how are Smith and Tony doing?"

"We sent them to the clinic at SOCOM. They are going to be ok but out of action for a few months."

Willis spoke up, "Some bad news Captain SFC Dale is KIA. We'll have to go back and retrieve his body."

"Sergeant Major I am sorry to hear that. I know he was a good friend of yours. No man gets left behind. We will retrieve his body."

"Roger that Captain, see you soon."

We approached the Tocabaga Bridge and

stopped next to the Iron Maiden where Captain Riley was standing. She walked over as I jumped out of the truck and said, "Sessions told me you would be coming in a truck of some kind, but this is a big ass truck. What the hell do you have inside Jack?"

"We have a truck load of BOTs and the two men who invented the dam things. Captain Sessions is expecting us."

"Ok you better get going and tell Sessions I'll be waiting for him when he gets off duty."

I climbed back up the ladder into the truck and Alvin commented, "You have some major security here with two Bradleys and one Abrams tank. The RCCD Units don't stand much of a chance against them in a battle."

"That's good to know because we were a little worried if we had enough fire power to knock out the robots. Keep driving straight down this road," I told him.

Carl answered, "The tanks have more than enough fire power. I told the FPF the Units were meant for police work not combat with the army."

As we drove into downtown Tocabaga

everyone was looking at the big black truck that had the words "Federal Police Force" painted on the side of the trailer. Tommy told Alvin, "Stop here and let me out. Dad I'll meet you here later, right now I need a drink, shower, and some rest."

"Ok Tommy see you later, have a shot of JD for me."

Tommy jumped out and we continued to Fort Desoto. The security team at the next bridge just waved us pass. As we pulled up to the Helo area Captain Sessions was standing there with 10 Rangers.

I told Alvin and Carl, "Ok guys we're here, welcome to Fort Desoto everyone out." We climbed out of the truck and Sessions came walking over with his security detail.

"This is the commanding officer Captain Sessions. Captain Sessions this is Dr. Carl Urban the BOT inventor and Dr. Alvin Sinclair his assistant."

Sessions didn't even shake hands but said, "You are both under arrest by order of General Harper, Commander of SOCOM, for acts of treason and conspiracy to over throw the US Constitution."

Carl yelled, "What do you mean under arrest? We're on your side now," as the Rangers grabbed their arms.

"See I told you they would arrest us," commented Alvin.

Leaning in close to Sessions I whispered, "Captain I think we should have Dr. Urban show us around the inside of the trailer. He has ten robots inside and some other secret equipment. He claims he wants to help us and more or less came along willingly."

"Ok, guards hold Dr. Sinclair here until we finish checking out this truck. Dr. Urban please show us around inside your trailer."

We followed Dr. Urban who walked over to the trailer and unlocked the back doors. The inside of the trailer was amazing, it was like a class five clean room, and there were ten Units standing along the walls.

Carl said, "Gentlemen welcome to my home away from home. As you can see here are the ten Units I told you about. They are all disabled at this time. The room in the back is my living quarters. We have various assembly and test equipment which I am sure none of you can understand. Over to the right are five controller stations and each station can control two Units at one time. Please feel free to look around but do not touch anything. I just gave you a gift worth about 50 million dollars."

I asked, "Dr. Urban where is the Master Kill Switch located and how does it work?" The Master kill switch was my main concern. If we can control the robots we can defeat them with out to much trouble.

"The Master Switch is located in a spot no one would think to look. It is right in front of your eyes but you can't see it. Anyone want to make a guess where it is?" He walked over to a small speaker sitting on a desk. It was a small computer speaker with a volume control and an on/off button.

Carl looked at us smiling and said, "The blue light shows the speaker is on. The on and off button does not control the speaker, it controls the Units. Look here, the button is clearly in the off position. That means the Units sensors are turned off. The blue light means the Unit sensors are off. If you push the button on then the Units become fully functional and the light goes off. Remember a blue light means sensors are off and no light means the Units are functional. I made it confusing on purpose.

"This is wired to a device that sends out a special UHF (Ultra High Frequency) radio signal from an antenna located on the roof of this trailer. This signal in turn boosts the Units receiver voltage. Putting it simply, inside the Units brain or CPU (Central Processing Unit) is a devise that is a small micro circuit and switch that detects the voltage to all sensors. When a voltage overload is detected it shuts off the power to the sensors.

"Every production RCCD is wired this way. It is my secret safety device. Everyone including Alvin thinks it is a normal system. It would be normal except I can overload the voltage using the radio signal which shuts down the sensors. It only takes an over load of 0.5 volts to turn off the sensors."

"How come the UHF signal isn't jammed or blocked like other signals?"

"There is only one frequency that is not jammed by the Units. I designed the system that way."

"Dr. Urban if we had a powerful transmitter putting out the same UHF signal we would be able to stop the robots anywhere in the USA?"

"In theory Jack that is correct."

Sessions looked at me and remarked, "Dr. Urban you need to provide us with that frequency so we can stop these Units."

"I told you, I am on your side and I will do that but first I need something from you."

Sessions moved closer to Carl, right up to his face and asked, "What do you need Dr. Urban?"

"First of all thank you for asking me. I feel like part of the team, the Ranger team now. Before we discuss what I need I would like to tell you what I could do for you besides giving you the signal frequency. I can teach your men how to operate the Units. I can show them how to repair and fix them. I can do research and development to make new and improved Units, thereby improving the Army."

"Dr. Urban that sounds very interesting," remarked Sessions.

"Now as for what I would like, I need your agreement not to arrest Dr. Sinclair or myself for any crimes committed in the past. I request to be the Senior Technical Advisor for the Army. I will lead the R&D and have final say so in any new

Unit design.

"I need an annual salary of $500,000 to start. Dr. Sinclair will be my assistant at a salary of $250,000 per year. We require free lodging on Tocabaga and free food. We also require body guards and request Sergeant Major Willis and Jack Gunn be our security team."

"Well Dr. Urban I need to discuss this with my superiors. I can't say yes or no at this time. Please give me a few days. While here at Fort Desoto you will have security with you at all times."

I stated, "Carl you don't need security on Tocabaga. I can promise you will be totally safe there."

Sessions advised, "Dr. Urban for today I suggest we put you and Dr. Sinclair in an Officers room for tonight. Maybe tomorrow Jack can find you a nice place on Tocabaga. Today we will bring you lunch and dinner to your room. There will be a security guard posted at your door so if you want to walk around he'll be with you at all times. How does that sound for now?"

"Ok Captain I am pretty tired and hungry any way. Is there any chance we can have a nice steak for lunch?"

"I'll try to arrange that for you and Alvin. Now please give me the keys to the truck." Carl handed over the truck keys without a word. I think he finally realized being a defector is not so easy.

I looked at my watch it was all most noon. I wanted to go home my ass was dragging. I am not as young as Willis or in as good of shape. Going more than one day without sleep takes a toll on your body. I just wanted a drink, shower and some food.

The security guards put the robot boys in separate empty rooms and Sessions, Willis and I went to the Captains office. We told Sessions everything that Carl had told us. We explained how we happened to capture him and Alvin.

Sessions asked me, "Do believe he is on our side?"

"Yes I believe him, but I don't know about Alvin. We haven't had a chance to talk to him."

Sessions suggested, "Why don't we talk to them separately to check out their stories. You guys take Alvin and I will talk some more to Dr. Urban."

"Good idea," replied Willis, to which I also

agreed. We went to Alvin's room and we began to question him. This gave us a way to cross check Carl's information and find out more about these robot geeks.

The Interrogation of Alvin was recorded as follows.

Question: Who invented the RCCDs?

Answer: Well actually Carl and I both helped to invent the RCCD Units. It was Carl's idea but I put it all together. I did all the assembly work and wiring. Carl always tries to take all the credit but he's lost without me.

Question: Why do you want to help us?

Answer: Carl told me I better help him otherwise you were going to kill us. What would you do in my shoes? I had no choice but to agree.

Question: What were the Units originally intended for?

Answer: The Units were intended for police work against criminals, terrorists, and so forth.

Question: What were the Units doing at Ellenton?

Answer: We were told to move the Units to Ellenton for crowd control and illegal possession of weapons. That's all the FPF told us. They didn't tell us they were going to kill everyone.

Question: What do you think about the FPF killing all those people?

Answer: I didn't like it but most of the people carried guns and would not surrender them. Some of them started shooting and then all hell broke out.

Question: What do you think about Executive Order 13603?

Answer: Basically I think it is good to control the population, resources, and eliminate the guns. There are too many guns and that is a big problem. I believe no one has a right to own a gun. Guns kill people.

Question: Do you think the current government lies to the people?

Answer: Yes it does but sometimes lies are necessary to achieve the goals of the state.

Question: What are the goals of the state?

Answer: To have a country where there is true equality. Everyone is the same and everyone makes the same amount of money. As one famous President said "You didn't make that by yourself, you had help from other people and the government."

Question: So the government helped you and Carl invent the robots?

Answer: Yes they did in a way. The government provided the funds necessary for our research.

Question: How does the card work?

Answer: The card sends a signal telling the Units you are a friend. The Units have a slot in the back and if you swipe the card the Unit becomes deactivated.

Question: Tell us about signal jamming?

Answer: The Units can jam radio and cell phone communications.

Question: Where are the Masters located?

Answer: The Master Controllers are located somewhere in Washington DC.

Question: How many Units are there at Ellenton?

Answer: There are a total of 300 Units stationed there.

Question: Is there any type of kill switch other than the card?

Answer: As far as I know there is no other

device to deactivate the Units.

Question: Do you believe in the US Constitution and Bill of Rights?

Answer: That document is so out dated it bores me. We need to write a new Constitution that reflects the modern times we live in.

Question: Is it all right for the law makers to pass laws that apply to us but they are exempt from the same laws?

Answer: Yes it is all right because they are the ruling party. If you want to be in the ruling party and have privileges then you need to run for office of some kind. Those in power deserve some type of extra compensation.

Questions: Why were you and Dr. Urban at Ellenton?

Answer: Ellenton was the first real field test. We needed to be there to see how the Units performed before the first major offensive action. Normally we would be back at the Research Laboratory.

Question: What do you mean the first major offensive action?

Answer: The first major offensive action is attacking Tocabaga. You didn't know that?

Question: Where are the robots being manufactured at?

Answer: They are being produced at the old Dali Art Museum in St. Petersburg.

We left Alvin and went to the Captain's office. He was sitting there waiting for us and asked, "What did you find out from Alvin?"

Willis replied, "We found out two major things. First it appears that Dr. Urban is telling the truth as far as we can tell. Secondly it seems that Dr. Sinclair is a true blood Commie. He does not believe in the US Constitution. I think he's a real danger to our security.

"Sinclair told us that Tocabaga is the major target of the FPF. Carl also told us that."

"Jack, do you agree with this assessment?"

"Yes Sir I agree with SGM Willis. Alvin is a real Commie. His thinking cannot be changed. It seems Urban saw the light and Alvin didn't for some reason."

Sessions told us, "I asked Urban the same questions as you did and he didn't change his story.

So we can only conclude he is telling the truth. However he is an ego maniac and I think he is dangerous. We will need to watch them both closely.

"Gentlemen if the BOTs are disabled I suggest we attack tomorrow at first light. I'll have Sergeant Cain send a drone to Ellenton to see if these things are moving around. If he confirms no movement then we will attack. We will leave tomorrow at 06:00 hundred hours. You will both ride with Dr. Urban and Dr. Sinclair."

I had to ask, "Captain why bring along the robot geeks?"

"They can tell us what equipment we should keep."

Willis asked Captain Sessions, "Sir if I may ask what is your plan?"

"We will take both Bradleys each one loaded with four TALOS warriors. The TALOS warriors will dismount and follow the BFVs (Bradley Fighting Vehicles) as they move forward eliminating the robots. The warriors will literally tear these BOTs apart. I want their heads ripped off and crushed. I want them made into junk so they cannot be used again.

"There will be four Humvees, each with four men, so that means four heavy machine guns. Willis you will be in command of the Hummers. You will split off and attack the work men and trucks using machine guns and rockets. I want you both to make sure the workers are captured or terminated if they put up resistance. You will take along Urban and Sinclair and ask them what equipment they need to keep. Anything we leave behind is to be destroyed. Is that clear?"

Willis and I both replied, "Yes Sir understood."

"The Iron Maiden will be along in case we need her. We will move in fast and hard. I don't want any robot left in one piece.

"After we take care of the one hundred Units on Route 275 we will move on to Ellenton and finish off the robots there. What do you men think?"

"Yes Sir Captain, that sounds like a good plan to me," Willis said while looking at me.

I replied, "I agree with Willis Sir."

Sessions added, "Men one more thing I think Alvin should be watched very closely. You are right he is dangerous and can never be trusted. Most of the hard core socialists never change their stubborn thinking. We are at war and war is hell. The very life of our country is at stake.

"After you take care of the work men and their trucks you need to retrieve SFC Dale. Tow the Humvee back to the check point. They will take Sergeant First Class Dale's body back to Fort Desoto.

"Oh by the way the dead BOT is being checked out by SFC Cain and SOCOM wants it flown to them ASAP. I haven't told SOCOM yet about the truck and the men you captured. I am going to ask SOCOM to do an air strike on the USF labs where they are making these things. We need to blow that place off the map.

"I have to phone General Harper inform him of our actions and discuss the request made by Dr. Urban. I don't think General Harper will look kindly on Urban's demands. I think the General will tell me to arrest them and send them to SOCOM. That's it for now men make ready and be back here by 06:00 hundred hours. By the way good work men."

We both answered, "Thank you Sir."

We walked out of the office and Willis commented, "Sounds like the Captain don't like the robots too much or Alvin."

I replied, "We've been lucky so far finding out how to kill the BOTs and nabbing the inventor. I think God is watching over us."

"I agree Jack. Let's go have a drink and get some rest."

Arriving at the bar we found Tommy who was telling about twenty people sitting there, the story of the FPF truck we captured. I just listened because I was too tired to talk.

Pulling Tommy aside from his story telling I told him, "Tomorrow we leave to attack the robots at 06:00 hours. We have to be at the Fort by then. The only ones going from our group are you, me, and Willis."

"Ok Dad, I'll wake you up. After this drink let's go home and see the wives and kids."

"Ok one more JD and we're out of here." Looking at my watch it was 2 pm.

Returning home my wife Hemmi was a little upset with me for being gone all night. I tried to explain why I couldn't call her. Ron and Jim Bo came up and we shook hands. The grand kids gave us both big hugs. Tommy and I took a hose shower, cleaned up and ate some lunch. Then we played catch with the kids and took a nap until dinner time. After dinner we both went to bed at 8 pm.

I was lying in bed thinking, something was not right about Alvin's story. I didn't know what it was exactly but it seemed fishy that he would openly state that he was pretty much a stinking Commie. I had to think of some way for an accident to terminate him. I don't want any stinking Commies on Tocabaga.

If my wife had any idea the number of times I put my life on the line she wouldn't be a happy camper. Funny thing is she has never asked me for any details. That's good because I could never tell her what I have done. I don't want her tainted by the bloody life of combat and have the nightmares that I endure.

JUNE 25, 2025

It was 05:30 hours as Tommy and I arrived at the Fort. We found Captain Sessions talking to Willis and the tank commanders laying out the battle plan. When Sessions was finished he waved us over and told us, "General Harper wants all the BOTs destroyed except for the ones in the trailer. He wants those taken to SOCOM along with Urban and Sinclair. They are officially under arrest now. Sergeant Major Willis and both of you will be responsible for them until we return."

While we were standing there Urban and Sinclair were brought out and handed over to us. Carl asked me, "Where are we going so early?"

"We're going to Ellenton. You need to tell us what equipment you require and let us know if there are any good workers we should have on our side." I made it a point not to tell him we were going to destroy all of his machines.

Carl replied, "They are called Technicians not workers. I only know of one Technician we could use. He has a lot of training and education that can be useful. He is very close to me."

"Ok Carl we'll see when we get there."

While standing there talking, dawn was just breaking. We were getting ready to mount up when out of the shadows walked 8 TALOS Warriors. We just stared at them in awe … they did look like Iron Man. It was the first time any of us had seen the TALOS Battle suits.

The Warriors stood in a straight line; they were all the same height standing about 6 foot 5 inches. The TALOS suits were a dark grey, brown, and black mixture of colors. These men had been selected to wear the TALOS after passing grueling physical testing and extensive training. They were the best of the best the Rangers had to offer.

The TALOS suit had the same outside reactive armor as the BOTs. Due to the shape you could tell a man was inside and this was clearly not a robot. I wondered how it must feel knowing you can pick up 500 pounds and run 20 mph. What does it feel like knowing you can walk threw a hail of bullets and they just bounce off of your armor. Wearing the TALOS you more or less become Iron Man the only difference being you can't fly.

The TALOS suit is a fully integrated system. It

contains computers, sensors, 360 degree camera, and antennas embedded into the suit to improve the warriors real time battlefield information. It has integrated coolers and heaters that can control the temperature inside the suit. It monitors the body temperature, heart rate, and hydration level of the warrior. The suit has an exoskeleton which operates by electrical - hydraulic servo systems which is powered by a new atomic battery pack that can provide energy for one year without a charge. The exoskeleton supports the weight of the suit and the equipment. The hydraulic systems enable the wearer to have amazing strength.

The helmet is round and angled with no flat surfaces so bullets would be defected. It has a small face shield with two eyes. It has a heads up display with thermal imaging and infrared. The operator can use a computer laser aiming device that never misses a target.

Looking closer at their weapons two men carried Mini 134 Gatlin guns, two had a 50 caliber COBB rifle, two men had in their hands an Mk 14 40mm six barreled grenade launcher and the remaining two warriors had M249 SAW light machine guns. These are all special weapons that are tied electronically to the built in computer laser aiming device.

The Mark 14 or Mk 14 40mm super six, was developed in 2012 and can launch grenades up to a range of 1,000 yards. It holds six grenades and can fire them in rapid order. It is a light weight weapon and is used by USSOCOM operators.

The M134 Mini gun is a 7.62x51 mm NATO, six-barreled Gatling gun with a high rate of fire up to 6,000 rounds per minute. It has rotating barrels with an external power electric motor. This baby shots a steam of fire that can cut trees in half.

As Captain Sessions approached them one of the TALOS Warriors yelled, "Attention," in a computer aided deep voice. All eight snapped to attention clicking their heels together at the same time. The first Warrior in line raised his helmet visor when Sessions stepped up to him and said, "First Lieutenant Fisher and the TALOS Warriors reporting for duty Sir."

Sessions responded, "At ease Warriors." The men took the standard at ease military position all at the same time.

"Do you Warriors have any questions about this mission?"

Lieutenant Fisher replied, "No Sir."

"If no one has any questions then everyone mount up," Sessions replied while holding his hand in the air waving it in a circle.

The 8 TALOS Warriors yelled in unison, "Rangers Lead the Way!" In a single line they trotted to the BFVs and climbed inside.

While everyone was scrambling to their vehicles I looked at Carl and Alvin and they were just standing there with their mouths open. I bet they were thinking the TALOS Warriors were bad ass dudes and very scary looking. The geeks were seeing what a real Army was like.

Carl looking at me inquired, "So what are you going to do with the TALOS men?"

"You'll see just get into the truck we have to move out now."

As we got into the Hummer Carl and Alvin took the back seat. Willis was driving, Tommy was on the M 2 machine gun, and I was riding shotgun. The convoy pulled out across the Tocabaga bridge. Sessions was leading the way in his Humvee. Next came the two BFVs (Bradley Fighting Vehicles), then the Iron Maiden with four Humvees in the rear. We were the last vehicle in line.

Here was the general plan of attack:

The drones confirmed there was no movement of any BOTs located on Interstate 275 or at Ellenton.

We would stop 800 yards away from the robots so the TALSO Warriors could dismount and follow behind the BFVs. The armor would open fire on the BOTs while moving forward ... not stopping. Once reaching the metal men the TALOS Warriors would move the exterminated pieces of junk to the side of the road destroying whatever was left and collect any weapons.

The Warriors and Armor will be moving south on Route 275 using the north bound side of the divided interstate. The Hummers under command of Willis are to speed ahead down the unimpeded south bound side of Route 275 when the first cannon shot is fired. We were ordered to cut off the technician trucks so no one can escape. If any resistance is encountered we will terminate them. Carl and Alvin are to advise us what equipment to take back. Everything else gets demolished.

After that is complete our Humvee is to speed

ahead and retrieve SFC Dale and the broken Hummer. We will tow it back to the check point where other Rangers will take Dale's body back to the Fort. Then we rush back and wait while mop up is completed on the 275 bridge.

Once mop up is finished we proceed to Ellenton with Armor on the north bound side of the highway and the Hummers on the south bound side. Drone recon shows there are about 300 BOTs standing idle there with no work men. So the Hummers will be providing security in case someone comes along out of nowhere.

We were assigned to burn Ellenton Mall to the ground. Soak it with fuel and light it up. The bodies left there could cause disease to take hold so it was necessary to cremate them all. Once all the robots have been destroyed we would return back to Camp Tocabaga.

A simple plan right, what could possibly go wrong. It seems at Ellenton anything could go wrong at any time. I am not counting my chickens before they hatch. The two trips we made to Ellenton turned into FUBAR.

FUBAR is military slang which means "Fucked up beyond all reason."

The tanks stopped one mile away and the TALOS Warriors dismounted. On the radio we heard Captain Sessions say, "Commence firing!" On his order the Abrams tank, BFVs opened up, and they all started moving forward.

The Hummers started to gain speed, and we reached the FPF trucks in about three minutes. The work men were trying to escape in their trucks. Pulling up to them we shot out their tires. If they didn't stop then they would be terminated.

Willis and the other Rangers were yelling, "Pull over US Army Ranges! You are under arrest!"

Alvin wailed, "Stop! You are killing our children! Stop it!"

I turned around in my front seat, looked at him and said, "There're no children here you fool. What the hell are you talking about?"

"The Units are the children! They belong to Carl and me. Please don't kill them!" Alvin and Carl were watching their children being blown to pieces. I laughed and so did Willis.

Looking across the divided highway the BFVs and Iron Maiden were blowing them to shit.

Robot pieces were flying everywhere. I saw an Abrams direct hit and the robot was an instant piece of burning junk from the 120 mm cannon. The BFV 25 mm chain guns would hit the BOTs and blow a big hole in the chest, cutting the metal men almost in half.

It was a blood bath except there was no blood but it looked like blood as the red hydraulic fluid flowed onto the roadway out of the tin bodies. Pieces of metal and robot parts were lying on the ground. They had no chance against the Rangers fire power.

The TALOS Warriors were walking along next to the BFVs picking up any robot parts and crushing them.

Carl yelled at me, "You didn't have to destroy them! You never told me you were going to do that."

I replied, "Those are the orders. The BOTs must be destroyed so they can't be used again."

Carl told Alvin, "Don't worry we can make more Units ... we can make more children." I thought these fuckers are really sick. They think these tin men are their children.

We rounded up the ten panel trucks and the big semi truck. All the men were ordered to get out with their hands up and stand next to their trucks on the drivers' side. Other Rangers were frisking them and using zip ties to cuff their hands.

Carl yelled, "Alvin put that knife down now."

I turned around to see what the hell was going on and Alvin had a knife holding it to Carl's chest. Alvin waving the knife at Carl said, "You lied to me! You lied and now you are letting them kill my kids."

I shouted, "Put down the knife, put it down now," as I drew my Glock and pointed it at him.

"No I am going to kill Carl and all of you for what you have done."

"I am warning you Alvin put the knife down now or you're going to get shot."

Alvin suddenly turned and stabbed Tommy in the leg while he was standing in the gun turret. Tommy yelled, "Dam it! The fucker just stabbed me."

Then quickly in one move Alvin lunged at Carl and I shot him twice in the back. He fell on top of Carl and didn't move.

Willis jumped out of the truck and pointed his M 4 at Alvin.

Tommy got out of the turret as I jumped out of my seat and opened the back door. Dragging Alvin out by his shirt collar I threw him to the ground. I looked inside and Carl had the knife stuck in his chest but he also had two bullet wounds in his chest from my gun. The bullets went right threw Alvin and into Carl.

Carl was still alive but fatally wounded and with his last breath he said, "Take care of my … Son."

"Tommy did you hear what Carl said?"

"Yes but who or where is his Son? Maybe he thinks a robot is his son."

The shots killed both of them. Tommy pulled the knife out of Carl's chest and asked, "Where did Alvin get this steak knife from?"

"They had a steak dinner yesterday and he must have kept the stupid knife."

Willis shaking his head commented, "The guards should have known better."

"Tommy come out here let me take a look at your leg."

Lucky for Tommy he was just stabbed in the thigh and no major blood vessels were cut so the bleeding was minimal. The serrated knife blade however made a nasty looking wound.

"You're lucky no serious damage was done but you'll be hurting for a while. I'll put some antiseptic on the wound and wrap it up. When we get back Doc Scott can check it out. "

After patching up Tommy we looked around as mop up was going on. The TALOS Warriors were throwing the dead BOTs to the side of the road and collecting the weapons. I watched one Warrior smash a robot head with his foot. All the robots had been demolished and the work men or technicians were in custody. It wasn't much of a battle for the TALOS Warriors but I was glad they were along in case any FUBAR did happen.

Willis radioed Captain Sessions and told him what had happened to Carl and Alvin. Sessions told Tommy and me to stay behind and guard the prisoners. Willis was to hitch another ride to go and retrieve Dale's body. He also told us to burn the bodies of Carl and Alvin as there was no time to bury them.

Tommy and I dragged the bodies to the side of the road, poured fuel on them, and sorry to say we torched them. We had no other choice but to cremate the robot geeks. I felt a little sad standing there watching Carl burn up. I had grown to like him a little. I made the sign of the Cross and said a silent prayer for Carl.

Tommy said, "Too bad Carl got killed, he seemed like a good guy."

The Rangers blew up all the trucks except for the big semi. Tommy and I were left behind to guard the workers and ask them a few questions. All was still as the main convoy drove away toward Ellenton Mall to attack the remaining BOTs.

Tommy and I now looked at the fifty prisoners sitting in the grass on the side of the road. They were huddled together in a large group. I went over to them and asked, "Who's in charge?"

One wise guy stated, "You're in charge boss man."

I walked up to him and kicked him in the face with my combat boot knocking him over and blood flowed from his broken his nose. Sitting back up he said, "What the hell did you do that for?"

I was not in a good mood since Carl was dead and Tommy had been stabbed and I replied, "Do you want another kick to knock some sense into you?"

Another man commented, "Hey we know our rights. We don't have to talk to you. You're a real tough guy kicking a man tied up on the ground." I couldn't help myself I walked up to him and kicked him so hard some teeth flew out of his mouth. He was knocked out cold.

"Now who else wants a kick? Let me explain something you have no rights. The President took them all away with Executive Order 13603. Now you are all under arrest for treason. Treason means the death sentence in war time and this is war.

"You men are responsible for killing a few hundred people at Ellenton Mall. So you are also under arrest for murder."

I noticed each man had a picture ID badge on their shirt. I told Tommy to watch them closely as I walked around tearing off the badges and taking the Unit control cards hanging around their necks.

They all had hate in their eyes as they looked at me. So I kicked a few more jerks in the face just to let them know I didn't like them. Then one man I looked at had eyes that told me he was looking for help. He appeared to be someone we could possibly talk too. His face looked familiar but I knew I had never seen him before.

I sat down in the Hummer and started to read the badges. The badges told their names and what title they held. The first guy I kicked was Joe the General Supervisor. The second one that I kicked was Nick the Weapons Expert and Sr. Technician.

Maybe one of these men might be a good apple. I was scanning threw the name tags trying to match one with the guy who looked friendly. I found his badge and to my surprise his name was … Dr. Carl Urban, Jr. … I thought holy shit this is Carl's Son.

Walking over to Tommy I said, "Look at this name tag."

"Wow that's interesting. Carl does have a real kid."

I walked over to the Supervisor named Joe and asked him, "What's in the trailer and who has the keys?"

He replied, "Nothing is in the trailer but spare parts. I don't know where the keys are shit head." Joe looked like a big strong guy about 40 years old with black hair and a small black beard.

Carl Jr. yelled, "That's a lie!"

Joe responded, "Shut up you little bastard. Your Daddy can't protect you now." Then I knew that was Carl's kid.

I told Joe, "You're pretty dumb and a slow learner. I guess that's why they made you the boss." Then I kicked him in the face once more. This time he didn't get back up for a few minutes.

I looked at Carl Jr. and told him, "Come over here." He stood up and walked over to me and I thought he walks just like his Dad.

I peered into his eyes and thought yes this is the man we can trust. He appeared to be about thirty years old and was about the same size as his Father. I took him by the arm and led him over to the Humvee about fifty feet away from the men so I could talk to him in private.

"Are you Dr. Urban's son?"

"Yes I am his Son. I saw you kill him and burn his body. Why did you kill him?"

"It was an accident Carl. I was trying to save his life. Dr. Sinclair was going to stab your Dad so I shot Alvin but he was on top of Carl. The bullets went right threw and also killed your Dad. I am sorry about that. I didn't know your Dad very long but he seemed like an ok guy. He was helping us."

"Why would Alvin try to kill my Dad they were best friends and very close if you know what I mean."

"Alvin freaked out when he saw us blowing up the robots. He called them his children and blamed your Dad. Somehow he got hold of a knife and started stabbing people. I tried to stop him but I was too late."

"How did my Father happen to be with you and the Army Rangers?"

"That's a long story but last night we captured him and Alvin. Actually your Dad more or less volunteered to come along and teach us all about the RCCD Units. We have his truck at the Ranger base."

Carl Jr. commented, "I knew something was

wrong when I woke up today and his truck was gone."

"To be honest we know Alvin was a big time Commie but your Dad seemed to believe in freedom and wanted to help us because of all the people killed at Ellenton by the Federal Police Force.

"Carl, are you a Commie? Do you believe in freedom and the Constitution of the United States?"

"I am not a Commie and yes I do believe in the Constitution. My Father taught me all about it because they stopped teaching that in schools years ago."

I grabbed a shovel and body bag telling Carl Jr., "Let's go bury your Dad."

I pulled my knife out and cut the plastic tie off Carl's hands. I had to use the shovel to put dirt and sand on the still burning body. The body fat was like a candle it would just keep burning. Using the shovel I scooped up the melted corpse and poured it in the body bag. It was a smelly mess. Carl Jr. had to look away and up chucked a few times. I felt remorse for the death of his Father.

While I was digging the grave I asked,

"How did you and your Dad get involved with the Feds?"

"Well my Dad invented the Units to make police work safer and help improve the situation for all people. The Feds came to us one day and took everything over. Basically they made us slaves. We had to do what they told us to do or go to jail. Alvin was happy about it because he was a Commie."

I was putting the last shovel full of dirt on top of the grave and Carl bowed his head. Carl said, "Thanks for helping me bury my Dad." I put my arm around his shoulder and gave him a little hug as he sobbed.

"We'll come back later and put a marker on his grave."

Walking back to my Humvee I advised Carl, "Ok you're not a Commie now prove it. When Joe told me there was nothing in the trailer but spare parts, you said that's a lie. Why?"

"First of all I hate Joe and most of these men. They're not good people. The trailer is full of guns and there are two Units inside that are Security Guards. Security Units have one purpose and that is to protect the technicians. They function

135

differently than the other Units. I know that my Father deactivated the sensors on all the Units that you destroyed. That's why they didn't fight back. I know how that system works since I helped invent it.

"The Security Unit sensors cannot be deactivated because we changed the design to protect us 24-7. These Security Units have a brain or central processor that controls them. They are real robots. The Units are pre-programmed, they do not have an operator or master. They think for themselves how to fulfill their prime directive which is our security. As long as you have a card and do not carry a gun you are safe."

"Your Father told us about them. What will they do if you have a gun?"

"The RCCD will order you to lay down your weapon. If you don't comply you will be shot or zapped."

"What if you don't have a card?"

"A card tells it you are friendly and if you do not have a card you are unfriendly. The Units central processor decides what to do. If it detects you are a threat or if you make any move it perceives as a threat it will kill you. If you walk away then you're not a threat. If you advance you're a threat. If you stand still or sit down it will watch you. So you need to have a card because the wrong move could get you killed."

"Can you turn this thing off?"

"No, unlike the other Units these cannot be turned off. The only way to stop them is to remove the power pack."

"Tell me Carl what happens if we open the trailer doors?"

"If you open the door they will jump out and scan everyone here for a card or weapons. I suggest don't open the door unless you have one of those tanks here ready to shoot them."

"Carl where are the keys to open the trailer?"

"Joe the Supervisor has them. He wants you to open the doors."

"Yes I know he does but I want to get those keys away from him. Carl stay here with Tommy." Tommy was in the machine gun turret watching the prisoners. If fifty men decided to attack us at one time the machine gun would mow them down.

Tommy watching me commented, "Dad be careful." I just shook my head yes and gave him the ok sign.

Carl Jr. asked, "He's your Dad? What are your names?"

"I am Tommy Gunn and my Dad is Jack."

"Jack Gunn was killed by al-Qaida."

"No he's still alive obviously."

I walked back over to Joe and said, "Joe give me the keys."

"I don't have them ass hole." Then he stood up right in front of me.

He was a good two inches taller than me and I could see the muscles in his neck. I knew he was strong but to me he was just another big bully. I looked up at him and said, "Sit down fuck ass before I knock you down! Give me the keys. We can do this the easy way or the hard way."

Staring into my eyes he grunted, "Let's do it the hard way."

Then bam … he head butted me hard right on the nose and then … bam … he gave me an upper cut with both of his hands cuffed together which knocked me back a few feet. My nose was bleeding and I was dazed from the upper cut punch.

Wiping the blood from my face I saw him break the plastic tie cuffs and two other men ran over to help him. I heard Tommy yell something as Joe reached out and grabbed me. I thought this ass hole is strong.

As he pulled me up I drew my Glock and pointed it at him. To my surprise he started to use the same hand gun disarming technique that I used to kill the cab driver in Mexico City. The method taught to me by a Navy Seal buddy years ago.

Now I knew I was in deep shit. This jerk knew how to fight, he knew hand to hand combat methods. I couldn't out muscle him so I grabbed his right thumb bending it inwards and down into what is called a thumb lock.

If you have hold of the thumb the hand and arm must follow it. Twisting his thumb back his arm turned and he dropped the gun to the ground. Now he used two hands to stop me from breaking his thumb. I quickly punched him in the throat as hard as I could and he was gasping for air.

I jumped back as the two other guys tried to

grab my arms. I pulled my Cold Steel fighting knife from my tactical vest slashing and cutting their arms. I heard them scream as they moved quickly back out of my reach.

I turned my knife on Joe and he suddenly had hold of my knife arm. He was too strong for me to stop and he twisted my arm almost breaking it making me drop the knife. Tommy yelled, "Duck Duck Goose!"

Years ago when Tommy was around 2 years old we played a game called Duck Duck Goose. When someone yelled that you fell to the ground. Last one on the ground lost the game. I knew that Tommy wanted me to duck so he could shoot the ass hole.

I was standing between Tommy and Joe so he didn't have a clear shot. The other two men were now as close to me as possible. Joe punched me in the face. Then he grabbed me in a bear hug and was squeezing the crap out of me. I couldn't breathe and felt the air being pushed out of my lungs as he pulled me up close to his ugly face. He was foaming at the mouth and his stinking hot breath blew on my face along with his spit.

The other men got behind Joe so Tommy

couldn't shoot them. But they didn't know Tommy is a great shooter. If he can see any part of your head or body he can hit it.

I saw one man going for my gun on the ground and I tried to kick him. I swung my head into Joe's face but my feeble head butt did nothing. The big bear had me ... then I remembered another trick ... stomp down with your heel on to the top of his foot.

I stomped and stomped and on the third stomp he let go just enough for me to slide out of his bear hug. As I was dropping to the ground I wacked him in the balls as hard as I could and he jumped backwards. This gave Tommy a clear shot. I heard six shots ... 3 double taps ... rang out from an M 4 and that meant three dead dorks.

Laying on the ground I looked around in time to see the last man fall and he had my Glock in his hand. I rushed over to him, grabbed my gun out of his hand, and promptly shot him in the head. I looked at the other prisoners who were all standing up wanting to get involved but didn't have the guts to attack.

Stepping over to Joe I noticed he was still alive laying there with blood pulsating out of two bullet holes in his chest.

His eyes glared at me as I put my gun to his forehead while saying, "You wanted it the hard way shit head," and I pulled the trigger … BAM. His head exploded blowing what brains he had out onto the road. One more dead bully.

I turned around looking at the rest of men and they made a move towards me. Tommy fired a burst from the machine gun over their heads and they stopped dead in their tracks.

I yelled, "If anyone else tries anything stupid we'll shoot all of you on the spot! Sit down and don't move a muscle!" Of course they all sat down like good little boys after the machine gun bullets whizzed over head.

I reached down into Joe's pocket and pulled out the keys for the truck. I picked up my knife wiping the blade off on my pants and slid it back into the scabbard on my vest.

I dragged my ass back to the Humvee and thought man that was close. The big jerk Joe could have killed me. He could have broken my neck. The whole thing was over in about three minutes but three minutes of fighting is a long time. I was really beat after that fight.

I fell into the front seat my hands were shaking and took a drink of water from my camel back. Tommy wet a handkerchief and wiped the blood off my face. Carl patted me on the shoulder and asked, "Are you ok Jack?"

Tommy answered him, "Yep he's ok. He does this all the time." We both started to laugh. Carl looked at us like we were crazy.

Carl advised us, "Those guys deserved what they got. They were real dirt bags. They laughed every time the Units killed someone at Ellenton. Now what are we going to do?"

A few minutes later I replied, "The plan was we were going to load these guys in the trailer truck and take them back to Fort Desoto. We can't do that since you have dangerous robots inside."

Carl suggested, "I have an idea. Since you have the security cards we are safe. All you need to do is put down the guns and stay away from this Hummer with the machine gun. Then we can walk right up to them and spray paint their eyes. If they can't see they can't fight. That's how I programmed them. If their eyes or camera is blocked they automatically stop."

"Let me think about that. If we put down our

143

guns we can just take a can of spray paint and cover their eyes. Won't they try and stop us from doing that?"

"No they won't if we do it fast. I'll do it, I'll paint their eyes. I have a can of black paint in the trailer. So first we need to let them out and I'll go in to get the paint. They'll be watching the work men and I will walk up to them with the paint can behind my back. I'll get real close and spray them quickly."

"Carl that sounds so stupid it might just work."

Tommy jumped in, "It sounds really dumb to me. I'm not putting down my gun. Carl are you willing to spray them?"

"Yes I can do it."

I asked, "What about their guns can we take them?"

"Yes you can take the guns after the eyes are covered but remember the Units have an electronic zapper in the left hand that can also kill you. We need to cover the arm with a piece of rubber after we paint the eyes."

"How do you work on these Units if you

can't turn them off?"

"They are voice activated. They have a voice recognition system. The three men you killed were the only people whom they would respond too. Once we have the eyes painted and the left arm covered then we can take out the atomic battery pack which will deactivate them completely. I can reprogram the Units to accept our voices."

"I think we should wait for Captain Sessions to see what he wants to do with the Units. I agree with Tommy I don't want to put my gun down either." I looked at my watch it was already 14:00 hours or 2 pm. We'll wait for Sessions and the TALOS Warriors to return before we do anything.

"Carl can these Units fight?"

"Of course they have a gun."

"No I mean can they do hand to hand combat?"

"No they have not been programmed for hand to hand but they will try to grab you if possible. Their hand can crush a coconut. Why do you ask?"

"I just wondering that's all."

I was thinking that when the TALOS Warriors come back they could have some real practice with these robots. I would like to see the Warriors' take on two Units.

I told Tommy, "It's past 2 pm where the hell is Sessions. They have been gone for 4 hours."

Tommy suggested, "Call him on the phone or radio."

I picked up the radio and pressed the button and all I heard was static. I tried phone but there was no signal. That means there are RCCD Units close by still in working order.

I asked Carl, "Are there any Units around here other than at Ellenton?"

"Not that I know of but the FPF is very secretive about what they do. So who knows, there could be."

"The phone and radio aren't working so there must be some robots close by us."

"No Jack, your phone and radio are being jammed by the two Units in the trailer. If you drive down the road 200 yards they should work just fine."

Tommy looking down the road yelled, "Hey here comes Sessions now!"

Arriving about a fifteen minutes later Sessions pulled up to us in his truck. He jumped out and said, "The mop up went great all the BOTs are destroyed and the mall was burned to the ground. How are you men doing?"

Sessions looking at the three dead bodies on the side of the road commented, "Looks like you guys had some action right here."

"Yes we took care of that situation but we have another problem," Tommy responded.

"What's the problem Gunn?"

"There are two live BOTs inside the trailer. They aren't normal ones. These BOTs think on their own, they have a brain. They don't have a remote controller. Captain this is Carl Urban, Jr. the son of Dr. Urban. He is also one of the inventors of the RCCD Units."

"Where the hell did you find him?"

"He was forced to work with his Father on the BOTs for the FPF. He is one of the men we captured. Don't worry he's not a Commie. He already told us a lot of information so he's on our side for sure."

I butted into the conversation, "Here's the situation if we open the doors on the trailer the robots will come out and shoot anyone with a gun. I collected these security cards from the prisoners. Anyone holding a security card and no gun will be considered a friend by the robots. Anyone with no card will be perceived as a threat. If you have a gun it will shoot you. They cannot be turned off."

Sessions took a drink of water and sat there thinking for a minute before he stated, "I would hate to totally destroy these because SOCOM would definitely want to examine them. So I suggest we open the doors and shoot out the eyes. Then we disarm them and remove the atomic battery pack."

Sessions looked at Carl and asked, "Will that work?"

"Yes that will work."

"Ok the TALOS Warriors will shoot out the eyes with their Cobb 50 rifles and the rest of us will back up out of range."

Captain Sessions called over the Warriors and told them the plan. They liked the idea as this gives them a chance to fight a BOT and not just do mop on already disabled robots.

All eight Warriors would line up about 200 feet away and Carl holding a security card would open the doors and move back out of the line of fire. Every Warrior would shoot at the metal men to see the affect of fire with the exception of the two Warriors who carried the Mark 14 or Mk 14 40 mm grenade launchers. Sessions didn't want them to blow up the robots.

Carl opened the doors and quickly ran out of the line of fire coming over to stand near me. The Units moved forward to the edge of the trailer and jumped out landing with a thud. They stood there scanning the area moving their heads back and forth. They looked at the prisoners and then the Units zeroed in on the TALOS Warriors.

One of the tin men spoke in a computer voice "YOU ARE IN VIOLATION OF EXECUTIVE ORDER 13603. DROP YOU WEAPONS NOW OR BE TERMINATED. YOU HAVE ONE MINUTE TO COMPLY." There was a one minute pause.

Then all of a sudden all hell broke loose as the BOTs opened fire on the Warriors. The TALOS men returned fire with the Mini Gatlin guns, SAW machine guns, and the Cobb 50. It was a blaze of bullets, a wall of bullets where hitting the Units and in a minute it ended. Fisher yelled to his men, "Cease fire!"

The BOTs were lying on the ground. They weren't even moving. The Warriors slowly approached them and so did Carl who went up and removed their guns.

The Warriors turned the Units over so Carl could remove the battery packs. The RCCD Security Units were now dead. Everyone walked up to the dead metal men to see the damage done by the TALOS fire power. The Gatlin bullets had done real damage cutting off one arm and almost one leg. The fire power knocked off the plastic reactive armor in many places making it possible for bullets to penetrate the body. The Cobb 50 bullets were right on target hitting them in the eyes. The robots blood or red hydraulic fluid flowed out of their bodies onto the road.

This test proved one thing the TALOS Warriors were capable of defeating any RCCD Units. They didn't need the tanks or cannons. The Warriors sustained very little damage. The reactive armor plastic paint had been chipped away but that could be replaced.

First Lieutenant Fisher raised his visor asking his men, "Is everyone ok?"

His men all replied back one by one, "A-OK Sir."

Fisher told Sessions, "Man that was intense. That was the first time we faced live fire. Everything went as planned. The suits worked as planned. I could hardly feel the bullets hitting me."

Sessions responded, "Yes that was intense but now we know TALOS Warriors kick butt. Fisher collect all weapons then load these BOTs and prisoners into the trailer truck. We're done here for today.

"Everyone else get ready to mount up."

Carl rode with Tommy and I back to Tocabaga. Sessions called me on the way back and asked, "What are you going to do with Carl? You know that SOCOM will want him to work on the robots and TALOS units."

"Yes I know, give me some time to discuss that with him. I think he will fully cooperate. We are the only friends he has now.

"By the way Captain doesn't it seem funny to you that the Rangers received a new deployment and the next day we find the robots at Ellenton planning to come to Tocabaga. I think we have a spy somewhere."

"I can promise you that no Ranger would be a spy for the FPF. You do have a point however. See what you can find out and report back to me. Talk to anyone you like."

"Roger Captain, I'll get back to you. Right now I don't even know where to start looking for a spy."

We made it back to Tocabaga with no further FUBAR. It was late and we were all beat. For the night the FPF technicians would be kept locked up in the trailer. Captain Sessions put Carl up in the Officers' Quarters.

Tommy went to see Doc Scott to have his stab wound cleaned and checked out. It wasn't a serious wound but you need to be careful to prevent infections.

Tomorrow I will try to find out if we have a spy on Tocabaga. If I find a spy they will be eliminated

*somehow. The TALOS Warriors proved they could
handle the job. We can feel secure knowing they are
here protecting us. I will certainly sleep better*

.

JUNE 26, 2025

My clan woke up early and after breakfast we discussed who could be a possible spy. We ruled out anyone that was an Army Ranger for the time being. We made a plan to find the spy.

First of all we couldn't tell anyone that we were looking for a spy. We had to be careful or we could tip off the spy that we were looking for him. We had no idea how many spies there might be on the island.

Jim Bo would check the Tocabaga bridge log to see who has been leaving the island and especially six days ago when the Rangers left for Georgia. Anyone leaving Tocabaga must sign out and anyone coming back in must sign the log book.

Ron and Tommy would ask around if anyone has seen unusual activity or heard of something out of the ordinary. Ron and Tommy would do this by going to the local bar and just talk to people that had too much to drink. They would also go to the local nightly fire circle held downtown. Everyone that attends likes to sit around the fire with a beer and bullshit. People discuss almost anything but mostly bitch a lot about the Feds.

I would check communication logs with the Rangers. The Army records every phone call or radio message for security reasons. We don't like doing that but it is necessary for our protection. All unusual conversations that may affect Fort Desoto or Camp Tocabaga are reported to Captain Sessions and myself. Since nothing was reported I maybe barking up the wrong tree. I had a hunch that if information was being leaked to the FPF it was being done so by phone or radio.

We made a list of suspects. People whom we thought were shady.

Scotty a loner who sold restate in the past. No one knows what he really thinks about the Feds. Scotty works out in the fields helping Maggie with the farming. He keeps to himself and doesn't make any trouble. Scotty carries a small 380 Colt in his pocket.

Chase is also a loner who always agrees with everyone but never offers his own ideas or opinions. We don't know which side he is really on. He is also a farmer and has one or two friends he hangs around with at the local bar. He smokes pot and drinks too much. Chase doesn't carry a gun.

Troy is an out spoken older man. He used to be an Electronics Engineering Professor at USF. Many college professors are liberals, progressive socialists, or maybe even Communists. His Son became a Commie years ago and moved to China. He has some weird political views and does lean toward being a liberal. I have never seen Troy carry a gun. He does electrical repair work for the island.

Ellen would do anything if it benefited her in some way. She can't be trusted to do anything. She has had many different jobs here and no one likes to work with her. Ellen smokes pot and is a hard drinker. She used to be a dancer in her younger days. She's a good looking woman but has no husband or steady boy friend. She would date anyone who wore pants. She is not the sharpest pencil in the box.

Johnny is a Tocabaga fisherman who always goes fishing by himself. Johnny would say one thing one day and then deny he said it the next day. Johnny would lie about it; whether it's intentional or not we don't know. He always carries a gun and he knows how to use it.

The question is which person had a background that exposed them to the Federal Police Force. Who had a chance to make contact with the Feds in the past? If we can find that out then we can check which name shows up on the communication logs or on the bridge sign out log.

Tommy and I went to visit Carl at the Fort. We sat down with Captain Sessions and Carl to discuss if he would like to work for SOCOM like his Father wanted to do. Carl agreed to work for SOCOM and thanked us for our support.

Sessions advised us the semi trucks along with 47 prisoners and Carl would be leaving later in the evening to SOCOM in Tampa. We bid Carl farewell and wished him good luck. I told him to come back and visit sometime.

Sessions reported that Smith needed extensive skin grafts and would be out of action for at least 4 months. He is in critical condition but he is stable. Tony received a broken arm and leg along with head trauma and would be in the hospital for at least 6 weeks.

SFC Dale would be flown to SOCOM for proper a Military funeral. Willis would go along with the body of his friend to attend the service.

I reviewed our plan to find out who is the Tocagaba spy with Captain Sessions. The Captain told his communication people to provide me any log information I wanted.

Tommy and I went to the communications office and poured over all the records for the past month. That took the better part of the day. The Rangers had some sophisticated radio and computer equipment. On the way out I noticed what seemed to be an old CB radio.

CB means citizens band which was popular in the 1970s. The CB was used mostly by truck drivers and had a transmitting range of 15 to 30 miles.

I asked the radio operator, "Is that an old CB?"

"Yes it's from 1979."

"Does it still work?"

"Yes it works." He turned it on and all we heard was static.

"Do you monitor CB transmissions?"

"No we don't because no one uses the CB now days."

Then it hit me maybe our spy used a CB radio to transmit information since that would not be recorded.

I asked Corporal Phillips the communications operator, "Can you turn this CB on and monitor it … recording conversations?"

"Yes but what channel do you want to monitor? There are 40 channels and since this doesn't have a scanner you need to pick one channel."

I replied, "If I recall channel 19 was the trucker channel. Everyone would go to 19 to link up. If they wanted to have an extensive conversation they would drop to another channel like 16. Monitor 19 and let me know what you pick up."

"Yes Sir we will do that. If I hear anything I'll call you right away."

"Thanks Corporal Phillips."

Tommy and I went home and found Jim Bo. I asked Jim, "Did you find anything?"

"Not a thing, nothing at all. Did you guys uncover anything?"

"Well actually we didn't find anything. I have an idea that our spy may have used a CB radio. The Rangers communication office has an old CB and I asked him to monitor channel 19. The question is who around here has an old CB radio?"

Tommy replied, "Who on our list would know how to use one? I think Johnny and Paul are the only ones."

"I agree with you unless there is someone else we missed. I suggest we go over the full list of people living here again."

We went over the list again and found one person we missed. He is one of the most out spoken liberals living on Tocabaga. He comes from long line of Government Union Members. I know he voted for the last President who got us in this mess and he likes the idea of the government controlling everything.

The one thing he doesn't like is giving up his gun to the government. I think that is the only reason why he lives here. He is walking a thin line but he knows Tocabaga is the only safe place to live. His name is Guy Allen but everyone calls him GA for short. GA moved here about 8 years ago from Georgia after his wife died from the flu. He has a distinct southern accent.

GA thinks he is a tough guy and he doesn't take shit from anyone. He stands 5 feet 10 inches tall and is about 180 pounds. He always carries his Colt .45 Commander and I am sure he would use it. He is assigned to the Tocabaga fishing crew because that's what he likes to do. He does have three friends who more or less think the same type of liberal crap as he does. I would never trust any of them with my life.

I told my spy hunters, "I want you to concentrate on GA and see what you can find out. Ron you follow him everywhere he goes for a few days. Tommy somehow check his car, boat, and house for a CB radio. Jim Bo you back up Tommy.

"A word of caution if you have a run in with him let me know right away. If the spy is GA it could be a very dangerous situation. Remember we have the "Stand Your Ground Law" so don't take any chances. If you think he is going to do something stupid like shoot you make sure you shoot first."

"The Stand Your Ground Law states that a person has no duty or other requirement to abandon a

place in which he has a right to be, or to give up ground to an assailant. A person is justified in the use of deadly force and does not have a duty to retreat if he or she reasonably believes that such force is necessary to prevent imminent death or great bodily harm to himself or another or to prevent the imminent commission of a forcible felony."

It was getting late so we concluded our meeting to spend some time with the kids.

It was midnight and my phone rang, "Hello Jack here."

"Jack this is Phillips we recorded a transmission from the CB about 3 hours ago."

"What did it say?"

"The message was in some kind of code. They just repeated numbers. I'll play it for you ... "21 11 21 0 7 9 6 24 16 8 0 15 22 21 7 0 7 12 24 0 26 7 0 22 18 20 19 7 0 11 14 0 20 12 18 13 20 0 7 12 0 8 12 24 12 14 0 25 18 20 0 7 6 13 26" ... that's all there is. You need to come over and hear this thing. I'll pass it on to SOCOM to be decoded if you agree."

"Thanks Phillips I'll be over first thing in

the morning. Don't pass the message to SOCOM right now we'll see if we can decode it tomorrow. Good night."

A code was being used by someone. What does the coded message mean? I thought we'll crack the code tomorrow and listen to the message to see if I can recognize the voice.

While laying in bed I thought GA has to be the spy. If it is him I made my mind up to kill him if he puts up a fight. He's the type of guy who would kill you by shooting you in the back. He is also the type to hold a grudge. Like me he believes in an eye for an eye.

That's all for now.

GOD BLESS AMERICA, LAND OF THE FREE AND HOME OF THE BRAVE.

Help me break the encrypted message. Email me your answer.

We are waiting for you to contact us by email to find out where Tocabaga is located. There is an email address hidden these chronicles. In case you missed it… tocabaga.jack@gmail.com

I will reply.

Jack Gunn

THOMAS H. WARD

DRAMATIS PERSONAE

TOCABAGA 4
TALOS WARRIORS

Bok Lam – A Chinese man and close friend of Jack's since high school

Colonel Turner – Commanding Officer of the Army Rangers based at Fort Desoto

Corporal Phillips – In charge of the communications office at Fort Desoto

Captain Sessions – Combat officer, commands and controls combat operations in the field

Captain Riley – Lady tank commander, girl friend of Captain Sessions

Dr. Carl Urban – The inventor of the RCCD Units and friend of Jack's

Dr. Carl Urban, Jr. – Son of Dr. Urban

Dr. Alvin Sinclair – Robot inventor and Commie killed by Jack

First Lt. Fisher – TALOS Warrior, Platoon commander

Farmer John – An old farmer saved by Jack now living on Tocabaga

Guy Allen or GA – Suspected spy living on Tocabaga along with Scott, Chase, Ellen, Johnny, and Troy

General Harper – Commander of the Rangers located at SOCOM

George Taylor – A nice kid who was bullied in school by Nick

Hemmi – Wife of Jack Gunn

Joe – RCCD tech. Supervisor a tough guy killed by Jack

Jim Bo – Husband to Amy and Son-in Law of Jack

Jimmy Smith – A bully from years ago

Leroy – The man who killed Jack's little brother Mike

Mike – Jack Gunn's little brother killed by a doper

Maggie – Wife of Robbie, who is in charge of the farming

Mr. Johnson or Famer John – Old time Farmer

Mr. Horn – Pig farmer and dirt bag who wanted to

kidnap Maggie for breeding

Nick – A bully from Jr. High School

Robbie – Best friend of Jack Gunn, a Tocabaga security guard killed by the FPF on April 27, 2025

Ron - Brother of Jack Gunn retired Navy Veteran

Rick – President of Tocabaga association, security team member

Sergeant First Class Dale – killed in action

Sergeant Major Willis – Ranger squad leader and security guard for Jack

Sergeant Cain – the Drone Master

Sergeant Smith - Army Ranger assigned as security guard for Jack

Tommy Gunn – Son of Jack Gunn and a retired Marine Scout Sniper

Tony – Bar keeper and sharp shooter for Tocabaga security

Victor Elway – An old farmer from Ellenton now living on Tocabaga with his friend Farmer John

Find these other books in

THE TOCABAGA CHRONICLES

Available on Amazon.com:

Book #1 TOCABAGA

Book #2 THEOTERRORISM

Book #3 WARM BLOOD – COLD STEEL

Book #4 THE TALOS WARRIORS

Book #5 THE QUISLINGS & ANDROKTONES

Or Buy The Complete Series:

THE TOCABAGA CHRONICLES BOX SET

For more books by Thomas H. Ward,

Visit his website:

www.ThomasHWard.com.